W9-BRU-662

A Matter of Trust

A Matter of Trust

DIANE NOBLE

GUIDEPOSTS
NEW YORK, NEW YORK

The author is represented by the literary agency of Alive Communications, Inc., 7680 Goddard Street, Suite 200, Colorado Springs, Colorado 80920.

www.guideposts.com
(800) 431-2344
Guideposts Books & Inspirational Media

Cover design by Dugan Design Group
Cover illustration by Dan Brown
Interior design by Cris Kossow
Typeset by Nancy Tardi
Printed in the United States of America

Chapter One

The first sign that Kate Hanlon's morning was about to turn topsy-turvy was when the tiny dog at her feet stopped munching his gourmet breakfast, tilted his head toward the front door, growled, then yipped wildly.

Not minutes before, Kate had padded into the kitchen, fed Kisses, and turned on the coffeemaker. It was 5:00 AM, her favorite time of day. Quiet. Serene. Undisturbed. A time for precious moments with God before the rest of the world noticed that the sun was about to proclaim the beginning of a new day.

Then the doorbell rang.

Kisses, Renee Lambert's teacup Chihuahua, barked again, his ears standing at attention. Like a miniature tornado, he spun around the corner of the kitchen toward the entry, lost traction, and slid several inches into the wall. He scrambled to regain his footing and then raced to the door, yipping and dancing on his hind legs.

Hurrying along just a few feet behind him, Kate tightened her bathrobe and hoped the predawn commotion wouldn't wake Paul.

A quick calculation of the time difference between Tennessee and Italy, and Kisses' yipping dance made the identity of Kate's early morning visitor no secret: Renee Lambert was back in town. And she had wasted no time coming to the Hanlons' to retrieve her "Little Umpkins" even though the sun hadn't yet risen.

With a sigh, Kate whispered a prayer for an extra dose of grace and reached for the door.

Then two things happened simultaneously: Renee barged in and gathered the Chihuahua into her arms, saying, "Did Little Umpkins miss his mommy?" and Paul came around the corner from the bedroom, barefoot, robe half tied, and blinking sleepily.

Kate had always been the early riser in the family. Paul usually didn't wake until the signs of dawn were well in place—a bit of birdsong, the scent of coffee brewing, and the palest hint of coming daylight.

Renee was still fussing over Kisses in the entryway. Kate reached behind her to close the front door, then met Paul's gaze just before he rolled his eyes. He looked immediately sorry, and Kate, knowing her husband well, figured his prayer for grace had come as swiftly as hers.

Kate interrupted Renee's kissy-cooing and gave her a quick hug. "It's a bit early, isn't it, Renee?" Kate said, trying not to reveal her impatience. "When did you get back?"

"Last night, but I couldn't sleep a wink." Renee sighed dramatically. "I know you're probably dying to hear all about the trip—especially because you were supposed to come with us. And do I have a story to tell . . ." She put Kisses on the floor and, without waiting for an invitation, marched to the living room. "But before I get started, I must have a cup of tea."

Kate avoided exchanging glances with Paul, then said, "Of course, let me put on the teakettle."

Renee plunked down on the sofa, and Kisses hopped onto her lap.

"Actually," she called after Kate, "I brought you a little gift. A tin of Earl Grey—loose-leaf, of course—that I picked up at the duty-free shop at the airport."

Kate turned at the doorway as Renee rummaged around in her oversized handbag. "That's so nice of you to think of us. Thank you."

Renee gave her a half smile as she stood, a small ornate English tin in hand. "Partly for you, mostly for me when I'm visiting." She handed the tin to Kate. "Now skedaddle," she said. "I've got stories to tell that can't wait."

Kate shot another prayer heavenward. It was now 5:18, and she hadn't even brushed her hair or had her first cup of coffee. She put on the teakettle and heard Paul excuse himself, presumably to brush his own rumpled hair and put on his slippers.

She poured coffee for them both and took a sip from her mug before setting it on the tray along with Renee's teacup and sugar lumps. As she waited for the teakettle to whistle, she warmed a small pan of half-and-half, then poured it into a creamer. Kate knew that Renee preferred real cream, but that was a luxury Kate rarely indulged in unless they were having guests. She and Paul had expected Renee to stop by to retrieve Kisses after their two-week "babysitting" stint, but not before Kate did her grocery shopping later in the morning.

"Don't forget the cream," Renee called from the living room.

The teakettle whistled, and Kate poured hot water into the teapot and carried the tray of coffee and tea into the living room. After she placed the tray on the table in front of Renee, who was sitting on the sofa, she excused herself and hurried to the bathroom to make herself at least a bit more presentable. As she passed Paul, he raised his brows and grinned. She couldn't help chuckling.

As soon as Paul and Kate were seated in the living room, Renee settled against the couch, took a sip of tea, and sighed again, this time even more dramatically. "What a trip!" Then she took another sip of tea, watching both Paul and Kate over the rim of her teacup.

"First of all, we were in the air for what seemed like forever yesterday, then there was the interminable sitting in the airport for hours on end because flights were delayed. You know how it is, bad weather, that sort of thing. It's enough to make a person never want to travel again, especially abroad."

She raised one brow. "But then one wouldn't get the culture and the enrichment that international travel brings." Renee closed her eyes and breathed deeply, dramatically. "Now, this is real tea." She sighed and then held the teacup out for Kate to fill again.

Kisses was once again on Renee's lap, looking straight up at her face. She slipped into doggie baby talk as she rubbed his ears. "Here I am talking about myself and the terrible flight we had yesterday, and I haven't even once asked about Kisses and how he got along while I was gone."

Kate smiled as she poured more tea into Renee's teacup. "Kisses got along just fine. He missed you, of course; we all did. And we're so glad you're home safe and sound."

What Kate didn't say was how from the beginning, her heart had ached to be part of that trip to Italy, especially to visit Assisi, the home of Saint Francis, a dream she had held for years.

"Well, now," Renee said, leaning forward, "I need to get to the best news of all . . ." Her face glowed as if she was holding a special and dear secret in her heart. "I've met someone. Someone wonderful. We met the very first day of the tour when we were in Rome." She fluttered her fingers and her blush deepened. "He's a widower, a retired professor of antiquities from Oxford. Can you imagine?"

Kate blinked and then took a sip of coffee to clear her head. "You met someone on the tour?" she finally managed to ask Renee.

"Oh, I met a lot of people on the tour," Renee said. "But this was different." She sighed again, this time even more dramatically. "This debonair man literally rescued me from getting drenched in the rain while I was shopping in Rome. We were on a city tour, with a guide, of course, in our coach—that's what they call their luxury busses. Our guide had the coach drop us in the very upscale shopping triangle, an area between the Spanish Steps, Piazza Venezia, and Piazza del Popolo along Via del Corso. You should have seen the place. It was glorious!"

She looked at Kate over the rim of her teacup, her eyes shining with the memory. "But I'm getting ahead of myself. I was about to tell you about Collin—"

"The man you met . . . ?" Kate prompted.

Renee's brow shot up as if to say, "Of course, who else?"

Kate took another sip of coffee. Paul cleared his throat, smiled, and did the same. Kate's heart went out to him. He still looked rumpled and somewhat sleep deprived, but when it came to his parishioners, even a challenging one like Renee, Kate's husband was a portrait of grace. Kate met his eyes. How she loved this man.

"He's English, a genuine aristocrat, if you know what I mean. You can tell by just looking." Renee's tone held a sense of awe as if she thought he might as well be a member of the royal family. "Collin Wellington. Oh, how I love those British names."

Paul leaned back in his chair, appearing to be in desperate need of more coffee. "Was he one of your guides?"

Kate rose to fetch the coffee carafe from the kitchen. She overheard Renee's response as she reached the doorway.

"Oh, goodness no," she said. "Our tour guides were all Italian, of course."

"I thought perhaps because of his antiquities expertise—"

Kate imagined Renee's raised brow when she interrupted Paul. "I'm sure he's much too busy to work for the pittance tour guides receive."

"Ah yes," Paul said.

Kate swallowed a smile as she rounded the corner with a fresh pot of tea for Renee and the carafe to refresh the coffee mugs.

Renee was so wrapped up in her tale, she didn't seem to notice the fresh Earl Grey. She went on to describe the new man in her life, rhapsodizing about the trip and about how he stayed by her side throughout the remainder of the tour.

"The amazing thing," she said, "is that it was as if we had known each other forever. In fact, he said the same thing. We were soul mates from the beginning."

She paused thoughtfully, then added, "He even helped me pick out a souvenir, a most glorious souvenir, that is a replica of a centuries-old urn. It was terribly romantic when he insisted we have our photo taken with the urn in front of the Neptune Fountain, right after the dear man followed our tour coach to Florence." She blushed. "Maybe I should say after he followed *me* to Florence. But I'm getting ahead of myself, aren't I?" She rushed on without pausing for a breath. "The Neptune, as you probably know, is in the Piazza della Signoria, in the heart of Florence."

"We would love to see it," Kate said. "The photo and the urn."

Paul nodded. "Indeed we would."

Renee's eyes brightened. "I assumed you would. Livvy was the one who took the picture, or it might have been Danny. Or even one of the others—LuAnne or Millie or even Mayor Briddle or Lucy Mae." She laughed. "Or maybe all of them.

"No vehicles are allowed in the piazza, so the coach parked a distance away, and we walked. But when we entered the piazza, cameras started clicking. There are glorious sculptures everywhere you look in the piazza." She sighed. "But the urn and Collin and, dare I say, *moi* were the stars of the show when we posed in front of the fountain."

She paused to catch her breath. "But enough about the photo. It's the real thing you want to see. It's in the car. Paul, I'm sure you won't mind going out to get it for me. It is truly a glory to behold. In fact, I have arranged for it to be displayed at Faith Briar."

Paul's eyebrows shot up almost to his hairline. "You have?" He pushed himself to standing and blinked. "You've had time to do that already?"

"Of course," Renee said with a laugh. "I called the other board members just before I came over here. They were half asleep, but all said yes. I was certain you would agree as well." Her smile was confident as she settled back and took another sip of tea. "With such a unique and gorgeous piece of religious art, it would be a crime to keep it to myself. Collin himself suggested it would be wonderful to display at Faith Briar once he knew how important my church is to me."

Renee handed Paul the keys to her car. While he was outside, she looked up at the framed print of the peace prayer attributed to Saint Francis of Assisi that hung above the piano.

"Well, now," she said with a decisive nod. "That's perfect."

Kate followed her gaze. "Perfect? My print?"

"Of course. It will be perfect to hang next to the display case spotlighting the urn." She turned back to Kate. "I'm sure you won't mind."

Before Kate could answer, Paul returned with a cardboard box. It was stamped with Italian words on the sides Kate could see and, in one corner, had a fancy floral design and what she assumed was the shop name where Renee made her purchase. He set the box at Renee's feet, went into the kitchen for scissors, handed them to her, and then sat down again.

Renee's expression softened as she sliced open the taped edges of the box, gently pushed Kisses aside, and then lifted the bubble-wrapped urn from the box and placed it on her lap. Kate and Paul exchanged glances and then leaned forward as Renee gently unwrapped the obviously heavy object.

She dropped the bubble wrap to the floor, then unwrapped a layer of tissue paper, until only the urn was visible.

"Ahh," she breathed, and Kate thought she saw moisture in the older woman's eyes as she touched the relief carvings on the sides. "It's more beautiful than I remembered."

She held the urn to the light from the sliding-glass doors, turning it this way, then that. It appeared to be made of alabaster and seemed almost translucent between the relief figures. "Oh my . . ."

This time there was no mistaking the tears in her eyes.

"Just holding it in my hands again reminds me of Collin." Renee's voice was barely more than a whisper. "And how much I miss him."

She held the urn out to Paul, her arms trembling with the weight of it. Paul stood to take it from her, then sat down again.

"It appears very old," he said, squinting as he examined the relief carvings. "Ancient, in fact." He touched one of the carvings reverently.

"It's a reproduction," Renee said. "But Collin told me it's one of the most authentic he's ever come across. He insisted I buy it." She paused, her lips curving into a rare soft smile. "And I'm so glad he did."

Paul handed the urn to Kate. When she took it in her hands, she noted that it weighed about as much as a stack of Paul's theology tomes. It was about twenty inches long, half again as high, and perhaps the same depth as height. On each side was a scene depicting something of religious significance. On one of the longer sides, two angels hovered over two bowed, cloaked, figures, one on either side. Around the figures, various animals had been carved: lions, sheep, wolves, and doves—some of which were depicted in flight, others perched on foliage carved into the corner of the design, and still others perched on the shoulders of the human figures.

Kate turned the urn to the other side. Only one human figure was depicted, a monklike figure with wolves on either side of him. One wolf stood on its hind legs, teeth bared, ready to lunge. On the opposite side of the monk, another wolf slept by the monk's sandaled feet. Behind them stood a crowd of villagers, their features and medieval clothing amazingly detailed. On the top of either end of the urn, cherubim perched, turned slightly so they were both looking down upon the monklike figure and the wolves.

"Francis of Assisi," Kate said as her smile widened. "It's the story of Francis preaching to the Wolf of Gubbio. It's not really two wolves but the same wolf before and after Francis' words."

"Yes," Renee said. "That's it exactly! We were there and heard about it firsthand. Apparently the wolf was terrorizing the town until Francis sat him down and had a little talk with him. His personality changed, and he was adopted, so to speak, by the townspeople, who cared for him until he died."

As she reached for the urn, Kate got up and placed it back in her hands, then sat down beside her on the sofa.

"There's even writing here that Collin says tells the story, though you wouldn't know it from me." Renee laughed and shrugged. "He's the expert on ancient languages. Plus he speaks several modern-day languages—French, Italian, and Russian, besides English, of course."

"Here," Renee said, pointing to the inscription. "It runs along the bottom of the urn, though in most places it's nearly worn off."

The lettering was so faint, Kate could barely make it out. As she ran her fingers over it, something bothered her about the piece, but she couldn't pinpoint what it was.

"What was this originally used for?" she asked Renee.

"It was a cinerary urn."

"Used for the burial of human ashes?" Paul asked.

"Yes, but remember, this is only a reproduction, so believe me, there are no remains inside." She laughed, turning the urn in her lap again. "I was concerned about finding somebody's ashes because of some mix-up, but Collin proved it was empty. I'll show you . . ."

She turned the urn so one end faced her. She pressed the cherubim's feet with her thumbs, then frowned when nothing happened. She tried again. Still nothing. She turned the urn to the opposite end and pressed the second cherubim's tiny feet. She tried to lift the urn's lid, but it remained tightly closed as if sealed.

She looked up at Kate and Paul with a puzzled expression. "That's odd," she said. "Collin opened it in a snap. He showed me there was nothing inside." She frowned and pressed the cherubim's feet again, shaking her head. "How strange. It's never done this before. It easily opened when he did it."

Kate and Paul exchanged a glance. There was definitely something odd about this urn. From the look on his face, Paul seemed to sense it too.

"Collin showed me the secret to getting it to open." She shook her head again. "I actually did it myself several times."

She again pressed the cherubim's feet, then moved her fingers, trying other possible releases on the box. After a few minutes, she looked up. "He even joked about it being perfect for transporting contraband back into the States."

When Kate and Paul didn't laugh, Renee frowned again. "It was a joke. He didn't mean anything by it. It was a joke."

Chapter Two

Renee looked across the room at Paul. "You don't mind, do you?" Again, her hand shook with the weight of the urn as she waited for him to take it from her. It was obvious she expected him to repackage it. Which he did, a smile that only Kate could see, playing at his lips.

As he placed the bubble-wrapped urn back in the box, Kisses jumped down from Renee's lap and whined, sniffed around the furniture, then headed to the front door and whined again. Renee gave Kate and Paul a waggle of her manicured fingers and chuckled. "I do believe Little Umpkins is telling me that nature's calling. Plus, I need to be on my way. I have a million things to do. You know how it is after being abroad." She glanced at Kate, half-regretting what she'd said. "Well, maybe you don't." She stood and pulled what appeared to be a new leash from her handbag.

"Genuine Italian leather," she announced as she held it out for them to see. "And the little hearts are made of eighteen-carat gold. I picked it up in Florence too."

The sound of Kisses whining and scratching at the front door carried toward them. Renee hurried along to let him out,

Kate trailing behind, with Paul bringing up the rear, holding the box with the repacked urn.

She stooped to clip the new leash on Kisses' collar, then stood and turned to Kate and Paul. "I nearly forgot to thank you for watching Kisses. I'm sure he was no trouble at all."

"No trouble," Paul and Kate said in unison and dared not look at each other.

No trouble except for the strict diet of homemade dog food Kate had to make fresh daily. Except for the heartbreaking all-night whining and yipping his first night away from Renee. Except for the fact that from the next night onward, he slept curled up between Paul and Kate, his loud snore keeping them awake.

"No trouble at all," Paul said with a grin. "Bye, buddy," he called after the Chihuahua.

Paul circled his arm around Kate's waist as they watched Kisses sniff a clump of grass, circle it a few times, do his business, then head back toward the front door, his tail wagging. It was obvious, in his mind, the visit wasn't over.

"We'll be back soon. I promise," Renee said as she pulled on the leash to lead Kisses back toward her. "Grandma and Grandpa will be happy to see you anytime."

As the big pink Oldsmobile pulled out of sight, Kate and Paul grinned at each other. Grandma was a name Kate would rather reserve for her grandchildren, but she couldn't help giggling anyway.

The phone rang as they walked back into the house. Kate glanced at the clock: 6:52. Parishioners usually didn't call that early. With a worried frown, she hurried to the kitchen and picked up the receiver.

"Mom?"

It was Melissa. And in that single word, Kate knew something was wrong. "Honey, what is it?"

"Mom, we need to come see you. It's important."

Kate detected a catch in her daughter's voice, and her heart skipped a beat.

"Of course. We'd love to have you."

"I know it's last minute, but we really need to talk to you and Dad. And Mom . . . ?"

"Melissa, is everything okay?"

There was a pause, then Melissa said, her voice stronger, "We're setting up appointments with . . . well, with some people in Pine Ridge. As soon as they're lined up, we'll be on our way." She hesitated. "Pray with us the timing will work out."

"Timing?"

"There have been some recent changes at John's office, and he's got a new boss. He's got this huge project at work he can't leave, not even for an em—" Her voice broke again, and Kate thought she heard quiet weeping.

"Melissa?" Had her daughter started to say *emergency*?

Melissa cleared her throat. "We'll explain everything when we get there. I promise. And I'll call to let you know when we leave. I just can't go into it now. Not until we know more."

As Kate hung up the phone, she slumped down in her chair at the kitchen table and looked up at Paul, who had just come around the corner.

"It was Melissa. Something is wrong, but she wouldn't say what." Kate repeated the conversation as Paul joined her at the table.

"We need to lift them in prayer," he said.

They reached across the table and held hands as Paul

began. "Gracious heavenly Father, we don't know exactly what to pray for, but Melissa and John are struggling with something. We pray that your loving arms would enfold them; that you would watch over them and protect them; that you would guide them and give them wisdom for whatever they face; and most of all, that you would give them your peace. Also, I pray, prepare us for their visit this weekend that we may be ready to support them in whatever way they need."

"Dear Lord," Kate added, "it is so natural for a mother to worry about her child. Help me, Lord, to put my trust in you and know that you will care for Melissa and John and Mia. Bring them safely to us as soon as possible, and give us the wisdom we need to minister to them."

Kate wiped the tears from her eyes as they raised their heads and looked at each other. "I know John has to fulfill his obligations to his new boss . . ." Kate's voice dropped off. "I just hope they can get here soon so we'll know what's going on."

"We've put it in the Lord's hands, Katie. I know we can trust him for the next few days. The best we can do is to keep praying."

"THAT URN IS NO ordinary souvenir," Kate said to Paul as they washed their breakfast dishes.

She checked the clock. It was almost ten o'clock, and between her concerns about Melissa's family and her growing doubts about the urn, her mind was whirling.

As soon as the kitchen was cleared of the dishes, she planned to try out a new cookie recipe she thought John and Melissa would like. If she couldn't help them tangibly, at least she could offer them some warmth and sweetness.

Paul picked up a plate, dried it, then reached for another.

"You're right about the urn," he said, then stopped and leaned back against the counter, crossing his ankles. "If I didn't know better, I would say it's the real McCoy, not a copy."

Kate sighed as her whirling mind settled. The look of Paul standing there, ankles crossed, idly drying the plate, calmed her. And talking to her husband about her nagging suspicions helped her put them in perspective. It had happened in the past; it was happening again. She smiled at him, thinking of all the reasons why she loved him.

"What?"

Her smile widened, and she shrugged. "Actually, I was thinking the same thing. About the urn, I mean. It's worn as if centuries old, and did you notice the hairline cracks?"

He nodded.

"Some looked like they had minute bits of soil in them, as if the thing had been buried."

"Which is what happens to a cinerary urn." He chuckled. "Of course, if it is the real thing, it's come a long way. By tomorrow it will be under a spotlight in that glass case Renee bought for the foyer."

"From dust to decor," Kate quipped. "Not to mention from ancient Italy to modern-day Tennessee. But that's not the only reason I want to take a closer look."

Paul grinned. "Let me guess. It's that Renee can't get it open."

She chuckled. "You got it. That's why I plan to call Renee to see if I can arrive a few minutes early for choir practice."

A brow shot up. "To try and open the urn?"

"Renee's pretty prickly about such things, but maybe she'll let me examine it a little closer."

Paul arranged a handful of knives, forks, and spoons in

the flatware drawer. "I'll miss our Saint Francis prayer, but I'm glad Renee thought of hanging it beside the urn display."

"I agree," Kate said as an unexpected quiver of disappointment filled her heart.

When she'd thought that she and Paul were going with the tour group, she'd read everything she could about Saint Francis, knowing Assisi would be a major part of the tour. She was so excited over the prospect of retracing his steps, she almost couldn't sleep at night. Even the prayer attributed to him that had hung in their living room since they moved to Copper Mill had come to life in a new way, its meaning even more precious to her than before.

Lord, make me an instrument of thy peace.
Where there is hatred, let me sow love.
Where there is injury, pardon.
Where there is doubt, faith.
Where there is despair, hope.
Where there is darkness, light.
Where there is sadness, joy.

O, Divine Master, grant that I may not so much seek
To be consoled, as to console.
To be understood, as to understand,
To be loved, as to love.
For it is in giving, that we receive,
It is in pardoning that we are pardoned,
It is in dying, that we are born to eternal life.

"Penny for your thoughts," Paul said, studying her face.

She smiled at him as she rinsed a few tidbits of granola from a cereal bowl, then handed it to him. "Melissa, of course, is always in my mind and heart, but this urn, Italy, Saint Francis, Assisi, are rattling around in my brain as well."

Paul sobered. "I know what you mean about the kids. When I least expect it, their faces pop into my head."

For a moment neither spoke, then Paul cheered her with that smile she loved as he flipped the dishtowel over his shoulder.

"Why am I getting the feeling a mystery is coming on? As in that little nipping thing that happens at the edge of your brain?"

Her spirits lifted with his lighthearted words. She flicked soapsuds at him. "Why do you always notice the direction I'm heading before I do?"

He chuckled, grabbed a handful of suds, opened his hand, and blew them at her. A few bubbles landed on her cheek. He gently wiped them off. Then he smiled into her eyes and kissed her on the tip of the nose.

"Because I do know you so well," he said softly. "And I love that part of you—your curiosity, your desire to find out the truth about things, your heart for helping friends . . ."

"I don't know about the helping friends part. I just want to get to the bottom of what's bothering me about this urn," she said. "This time it's strictly curiosity."

"Uh-huh," Paul said, still grinning. "We'll see."

KATE CREAMED THE BUTTER and eggs, the mixer whirring. She measured the dry ingredients, then gradually stirred them into the mix as she moved her thoughts from Melissa's phone call to Renee and her urn. Paul was probably right. Maybe her curiosity didn't have as much to do with the urn as it did with Renee's vulnerability.

She smiled as she stirred in some oatmeal and almond

extract. *Renee* and *vulnerability* were two words she'd not often connected in the same breath.

She stirred in some butterscotch chips, put her hand on her hip and looked into the rich dough. The almond fragrance was delicious. She went over to the refrigerator for some chopped walnuts, brought them back and measured out a cupful.

After stirring them in, she dropped dollops of the dough onto a baking sheet, then placed the sheet in the preheated oven.

The idea of Renee being vulnerable hit her again . . . along with images of the urn, thoughts of the secret steps that no longer opened it, and Collin's supposed joke about it being a good place to hide contraband.

Yes, it seemed Renee had gotten into something more complicated than she'd anticipated. Kate didn't know why or how, but Paul was right: she had a heart for helping friends. And no matter how the woman could irritate her, Renee was Kate's friend.

AS PLANNED, Kate arrived at Renee's a half hour ahead of the other choir members. Renee's mother, Caroline, opened the door and let her in, frowning as Kisses yipped, jumped, and ran in circles when he saw Kate.

Renee came around the corner in a cloud of Estée Lauder's Youth-Dew. "Dear, when you called, you didn't mention you'd be here *this* early."

"Well, I'd really hoped to spend a few extra minutes with your beautiful urn."

Renee brightened. "That's what you said, but honestly, I'm rushing around getting ready for the others . . ." She let the words fall off dramatically. "I was just putting on tea."

Kate followed her into the living room, where the urn was

prominently displayed on the coffee table. It seemed to almost glow in the nearby lamplight.

"May I take another look?" She glanced at Renee, who nodded as Kate knelt beside the glass table.

Behind Renee stood a scowling Caroline. "Urn-*schmurn*," she said. "And I suppose you've heard all about Renee's romantic Mr. Urn?"

"Mother, please," Renee said, her lips tight. "His name is Collin Wellington."

Caroline rolled her eyes and, turning, made her way out of the room with what Kate thought was an exaggerated hobble.

Kate turned her attention back to the urn. Several things about it intrigued her: the strange symbols that ribboned the bottom, depicting some sort of ancient language; a soil-like substance in the hairline fractures that covered the entire piece; and the secret steps to opening the urn that Renee couldn't duplicate.

And why would Collin Wellington even joke about the urn being a place to hide contraband? She couldn't get her mind around all that might mean.

She had to open the urn.

"The secret steps to opening the urn," she said to Renee, standing again. "Have you tried them again?"

"Oh yes. Many times." Renee sat down on the sofa and lifted the urn onto her lap. As if unable to resist trying one more time, she fiddled with the feet of the cherubim, gently pulling, then pushing, this way and that. Nothing.

"May I try?"

Renee shot her a quizzical look. "Why the sudden interest?"

Kate sat down next to her. "I think it's strange that you once were able to open it, and now you can't."

Renee sighed. "Well, I can understand that. I feel the same way." She lifted the urn and placed it on Kate's lap.

"It has something to do with the feet. And I swear I'm doing the same thing Collin showed me." She showed Kate the exact steps.

Kate tried various movements with the figures, the cherubim as well as Saint Francis and the wolves on one side and the cloaked figures on the opposite side.

She shook her head slowly. "You're right. It seems locked fast."

"Strange, I know. But there must be something I've overlooked," Renee said with a shrug. "Though it's not like me to overlook anything."

Kate heard a car pull up and park outside and glanced at her watch. Choir practice was about to begin. Renee started for the entry door.

"Wait," Kate said, catching up with her. "Was the urn out of your sight anytime after you purchased it?"

"That goes without saying," Renee said with a sniff. Her penciled eyebrows arched. "I had to check it for the flight home."

"Aside from that, I mean," Kate said. "Did anyone have access to it—in a hotel room, on the tour bus, that sort of thing?"

"Tour *coach*," she corrected, then added, "You're wondering if I left the urn unprotected so someone could place contraband inside and seal it up again?"

A loud rap interrupted them, and Renee again headed toward the entry door. Just before she opened it, she turned back to Kate. "The answer is that nobody had access to it, that I know of, anyway. I certainly didn't carry it around with me throughout the rest of the tour. With its weight and size, can you imagine I could do such a thing?" She let out an irritated sigh. "Besides, I really didn't think of it as valuable to anyone but me. As time went on, its value increased—to me—but because of Collin, not because of any kind of intrinsic value the urn might have."

She paused as the rapping at the door sounded again. "Even Collin kept it in his car for a few days at the end of the trip so I wouldn't have to bother taking it in and out of hotels."

Collin Wellington had it in his possession?

A million questions hit Kate's brain at once, but before she could ask a single one, Renee had opened the door, and the Faith Briar choir members poured through.

THAT NIGHT as Kate finished her prayers and lay in bed, she thought about Melissa, John, and little Mia. All day, their names had been on her lips in prayer more times than she could count. She lifted them again before the Father, asking him to watch over them.

Just as she was drifting off, the image of Renee's urn floated back into her mind. At first she pictured the relief figures of Saint Francis of Assisi, the Wolf of Gubbio, and the two cloaked figures on the opposite side of the urn. None of the depictions bothered her. Then she thought about the almost invisible ancient writing, which was a puzzle.

But nothing bothered her as much as the secret steps to opening the urn and the cherubim that guarded them. The box had been out of Renee's sight for hours, even days, before her flight home, and the urn wouldn't open once it was again in her possession.

Chapter Three

The next morning, Kate settled into her rocker to read her Bible and spend time in prayer. Her heart was still troubled by the emotion she'd heard in her daughter's voice the day before. It reminded her of when Melissa was a frightened toddler and cried out "Mama" in the middle of the night.

"Father," she prayed, "wrap your loving arms around Melissa, John, and little Mia. Whatever it is they're facing, strengthen them, guide them, and may they know you are with them."

She opened her Bible to the Psalms, searching for words that would bring her comfort. Her gaze fell on Psalm 59:16–17, and the worries subsided as she began to read.

But I will sing of Your power;
Yes, I will sing aloud of Your mercy in the morning;
For You have been my defense
And refuge in the day of my trouble.
To you, O my Strength, I will sing praises;
For God is my defense,
My God of mercy.

Kate settled back and smiled. *I will sing aloud of Your mercy in the morning . . .*

"Yes," she whispered, "my Refuge, my Strength, my God of mercy . . . and peace. I'll sing . . ."

A song came to her, and she hummed the words, taking comfort in them. *"He is our peace, who has broken down every wall; He is our peace, He is our peace. Cast all your cares on Him, for He cares for you; He is our peace . . ."*

Still humming, she went into the kitchen and poured a mug of coffee. No matter what was ahead, no matter the troubles—whether large or small—her Lord was her peace.

Before heading back into the living room, she glanced at the clock: 7:30. The kids would be awake by now. She promised herself she wouldn't pry, but she couldn't help dialing their number.

The phone rang several times before clicking over to voice mail. After John's warm greeting, Kate swallowed hard and said, "Dear ones, your dad and I just wanted you to know how much you're loved. We're praying for you constantly. Call us if there's anything else we can do."

She hesitated, then added, her voice shaky, "We can't wait to see you. Hugs and love to you all."

She stood by the phone for several minutes, hoping Melissa would call right back. Maybe she'd been in the shower or giving Mia her bath. Or maybe they were sleeping in a little longer than usual.

But Melissa didn't return the call.

When the phone did ring a half hour later, her heart skipped a beat, and she made a dash for it, picking it up on the third ring.

It was Livvy. A very excited Livvy.

"Kate, my first column is in today's *Chronicle*!"

"About the trip?"

"One and the same."

Kate could almost hear her friend's smile through the phone.

"That's great. I can't wait to read the whole series of them. I know I'll feel like I was right there with you when I read them. Speaking of which . . ."—Paul came around the corner from the living room, waving a section of the *Copper Mill Chronicle*—"Paul just came in with the paper."

Livvy laughed. "Your husband's timing always seems to be perfect."

A wave of nostalgia for the trip nipped at her heart, but she quickly pushed it from her mind, though not before thinking, *Paul's timing perfect?* As much as she loved her husband, she would always wonder why he hadn't raised the red flag about their finances before she had launched herself well into planning the trip to Italy, studying the life of Saint Francis, mapping out their adventures . . .

The friends agreed to meet for lunch at the diner, then said their good-byes.

Sitting at the table, Paul placed the cordless receiver in front of him then unfolded the paper with a rattle and a snap. Kate swallowed a smile. It wasn't often that her husband showed any absent-minded tendencies, but his carrying the bedroom phone to the kitchen was a little strange to say the least.

"Look at this." Paul picked up the paper for closer scrutiny. "Renee and Collin made the first page. With the urn." He read the caption beneath the photo.

> Renee Lambert of Copper Mill with Collin Wellington of Oxford, England, in front of the famous Neptune

> Fountain in Florence, Italy. Renee is holding a replica of an ancient urn, which Wellington, a professor of antiquities, helped her purchase not far from where the photo was taken. The urn will be on display in the foyer of Copper Mill's Faith Briar Church.

Kate walked to the table and peered over Paul's shoulder. "He's a nice looking man," she said, bending closer. "He looks a bit like that actor, what's his name?"

Paul grinned up at her. "I'll need a clue."

"British. Played C. S. Lewis . . ."

"Anthony Hopkins."

"That's it," Kate said. "Collin looks just like him." She paused, then added, "Oh, what a romantic setting for a photo . . ." Her eyes misted, and she didn't finish.

Paul looked up, studied her face, then reached for her hand. "I know how badly you wanted to go, Katie. I'm so sorry . . ."

She managed a smile as she sat down beside him. "It's okay. Honest, it is. Now, let's read the article. I've rarely heard Livvy sound so excited . . ."

> The Trip of a Lifetime
> by Olivia Jenner
>
> I've long dreamed of going to Italy. And as Alitalia flight 743 made its final approach to the Rome airport above the Tyrrhenian Sea, I gazed down at the terra-cotta rooftops, the fields of green in the distance, the stunning ancient city, sparkling in the late-afternoon sun, and I realized my dream was actually coming true.
>
> We were still struggling with jet lag when our tour guide met us outside customs. She held up a sign that

said "Triple T Tours," and we made our way toward her, glad to be in such capable hands in a foreign country.

Our tour group was made up entirely of people from Tennessee. (Triple T stands for Tennesseans Tour Tuscany.) Besides my husband, Danny, and myself, others hailing from Copper Mill included LuAnne Matthews, Millie Lovelace, Renee Lambert, and Mayor Briddle and his wife, Lucy Mae.

Though we didn't know those travelers from outside our little town when the tour began, we all soon became friends; that's what happens when you spend hours together on a luxury coach, take meals together, tour together, and shop together.

One other significant member of our group, however, did not appear until our first full day in Rome. And he was definitely not from Tennessee, though word has it he may be visiting here soon. But I'm getting ahead of myself . . .

After getting us checked in and settled a bit in our hotel, our guide took us to get a taste of shopping in one of Rome's upscale boutique and fashion districts. It's known as the shopping triangle, an area along Via del Corso, just next to the famous Spanish Steps.

The group quickly spread out to window-shop, though a few of us did more than *ooh* and *ahh* over the beautiful clothing, jewelry, and leather goods. Renee Lambert took the stop very seriously.

Her arms were soon loaded with decorative bags filled with her purchases. She was crossing the triangle when the driver of the Triple T coach sounded the horn to signal it was time to leave. At the same time, the heavy-laden clouds that had been threatening storms all day, gave way, the wind kicked up, and rain began to pour.

Renee quickly became drenched, and in her hurry to open her umbrella and pull on her raincoat, she dropped her bags. Cars and motorbikes zipped by, drivers honking and yelling for her to get out of the way.

Before any of us could reach her to help, along came a knight in shining armor. The man swept his stylish rainproof cape over Renee's head and guided her out of harm's way. Those of us watching from under a nearby awning let our jaws drop in awe. We half expected him, with a grand flourish, to place his cape over the quickly rising puddles for her to step across.

He saw her safely to our coach. At some point during the grand sweep of his cape, he had almost magically retrieved the dropped packages. He handed them to her as they said their good-byes, and Renee's "knight," whose name we later learned was Collin Wellington, disappeared into the crowd.

As you have surely guessed, this wasn't the last we saw of Collin Wellington. We ran into him nearly every day of our remaining time in Italy—from Florence to Assisi to Siena and villages large and small in between—as it seemed this professor of antiquities had chosen an Italian journey similar to ours, which was our gain. He added depth to our understanding of the sights, and before too long, we had practically adopted him as one of Triple T's own.

Livvy's article went on to describe the highlights of Rome: St. Peter's Basilica, the Coliseum, the Forum, and the

Catacombs. Kate drank in every word, imagining the wonder of seeing the places she'd only read about.

Kate felt Paul's gaze on her, and her cheeks flushed as she looked up.

He gently squeezed her hand. "I can see it in your eyes," he said quietly.

She raised an eyebrow.

"I can see how much you wanted to be there with Livvy and all the rest."

She stood and kissed his cheek. "I wanted mostly to be there with you," she said. "Maybe someday—"

The telephone rang, interrupting her thoughts and words.

Paul ignored the kitchen phone and reached for the cordless handset. As someone on the other end of the connection spoke rapidly, Paul stood and hurried into the living room.

Kate heard him say, "Of course, that's perfectly understandable. I'll take care of it as soon as I can."

When he returned to the kitchen, his face was flushed, and he seemed to avoid her questioning gaze.

"Is it a church emergency? Is everything okay?"

He stared at her for a moment, biting his lower lip and looking uncomfortable. "It's something I must keep confidential," he finally said. "Also something I need to take care of right away."

He gave her a quick kiss, then hurried from the kitchen toward the front door.

Kate followed a few steps behind. "But Paul . . ."

The door had already closed by the time she got the words out. Moments later, she heard him start his pickup truck and back into the street.

Chapter Four

Kate thought about Paul's strange phone call as she dressed for the errands she needed to run that morning. In all their years of marriage, they had never kept secrets from each other. On the other hand, if someone wanted him to keep something confidential, she knew he would do just that. What puzzled her was the flush that rose in his cheeks and the way he seemed to avoid her eyes. But then, maybe she had just imagined both.

An hour later, his behavior was still on her mind as she pulled into the church parking lot. Paul's pickup was in its usual spot, so Kate wondered if whatever had caused him to hurry out of the house had been taken care of—unless it had something to do with Faith Briar and one of the parishioners.

She entered the foyer and then stopped with a gasp. Renee's exhibit was breathtakingly simple and beautiful. The cabinet was as tall as a grandfather clock with a cherry-wood frame and glass panels. A single glass shelf graced the interior.

But it wasn't the cabinet that made Kate stop in awe. It was the urn itself, centered on the glass shelf. It seemed to be glowing with light from inside.

It was an optical illusion, of course, obviously caused by the spotlight above the urn at the top of the cabinet.

Almost reverently, Kate moved toward the glass case. How could something this magnificent be a replica? She wanted to get a closer look, hold it in her hands again.

Not surprisingly, the cabinet was locked.

Kate headed immediately to Paul's office. Surely Renee had left a key with either Paul or Millie Lovelace, the church secretary.

Millie was sitting in her usual spot just outside Paul's office, talking on the phone, and with a little nod and gesture, she indicated that Paul was in his office.

Kate peeked in, at the same time giving a soft rap. When Paul looked up, his eyes brightened.

He stood, his grin spreading. "What brings you here?"

"I thought I'd have another look at the urn." She gave him a sheepish smile. "I know I may be getting a bit obsessive about this, but I just can't help it. There's something intriguing about the urn that compels me to study it. Plus, I wanted to see how it looks now that it's in place."

Paul chuckled. "I must admit I had my doubts when Renee first mentioned putting it on display here, but it looks very nice in the foyer—almost as if it belongs."

"Want to come back out with me to have another look?" Kate lowered her voice and glanced toward the door. "I don't want any rumors to get started. And I especially don't want anything to get back to Renee, but my doubts about this urn just won't go away."

A shadow crossed Paul's face, but in a heartbeat it was gone. "I can't, Katie. I'm expecting a phone call."

As if on cue, Millie appeared in the doorway. Kate wondered how long she'd been standing there. "Call on line one, Pastor."

Paul's face turned pink again, just as it had earlier that morning. He gestured to the door, looking pleasant enough, but his words stung. "I'm sorry, Kate. If you'll excuse me?"

Kate blinked in surprise. She'd never been dismissed from her husband's office before. She felt her own cheeks flush. "Of course, Paul. I'll be in the foyer, if you want to join me later."

But he was listening intently to the person on the other end of the line and didn't answer. And she hadn't had a chance to ask about the locked cabinet.

She hurried toward Millie's desk, becoming more puzzled with each step.

Millie looked up with a smile as Kate asked about the key. "We do have one, but only Pastor Paul, Renee, you, and I can know about it. Renee has one of her own, of course."

Millie unlocked a metal filing cabinet, rummaged around inside the top drawer with a few clangs, bangs, and metallic jangles, then pulled out a small metal box filled with staples, paper clips, double-A batteries, rubber bands, and keys.

"Aha," she said, holding up a small brass key on a jeweled ring with a miniature photo of Kisses dangling from it.

Kate couldn't help smiling; it was Renee all the way.

"This is it." Millie handed the key to Kate. "Don't forget to return it."

A few minutes later, in front of the case once more, Kate inserted the key, turned it, pulled open the door, and reached for the urn. Again she was struck by its surprising weight. There were no chairs in the foyer, so she gingerly carried the urn through the doors into the sanctuary. She chose a pew near one of the side windows with plenty of sunlight, and she sat down.

The cracks were even more evident in this bright light than they had been before. She moved her fingertips across the pattern of lines, trying to determine if they were painted on to make the piece look ancient, or if they were actually hairline cracks. She couldn't tell without a magnifying glass.

She turned the piece to examine the side with the two robed figures and the animals. She let her fingers lightly trace over the faces, and then smiled as it came to her. The one with the covered head was female; the other, with tonsured hair, was male. Francis and Clare. *Of course.*

Over the past several months, she had read everything she could find about both Saint Francis and Saint Clare. She knew that Clare was one of Francis' early followers and that she had quickly embraced his determination to live the gospel simply with great joy and a full heart.

Kate's gaze drifted to the cherubim, and she couldn't help trying to mimic the steps Renee had shown her. She hadn't expected it to open, and it didn't. Squinting in thought, she sat back to study the piece, wondering why it intrigued her so.

Was it because the urn was supposedly a replica of an ancient artifact but appeared to her to be older than Methuselah? Or was it because of her niggling concerns about how Collin showed up out of the blue, a so-called white knight riding to the rescue of rain-drenched Renee? Or was it that the urn could no longer be opened—and that Collin had made a seemingly offhand comment about hiding contraband?

Kate studied the line of strange characters or letters that ran below the figures in carved relief. She squinted, holding the piece closer, regretting that the etched lettering was worn to the point of being barely visible.

They were obviously characters or letters in some ancient

language. She had seen similar lettering, but for the life of her, she couldn't think of where or when. She would need to do a bit of sleuthing to figure that out, perhaps in one of the books she had picked up on Francis, or from a college class in ancient history decades ago.

She stood and started down the outside aisle to the back of the church. Before she reached the foyer, one of the double doors opened, and Paul stepped through.

"There you are!" He held the door open for Kate, and she stepped into the foyer.

She raised an eyebrow. "That must have been some important phone call." She wanted to bite her tongue for letting the complaint slip out and hoped her tone came out more gracious than it sounded to her. It apparently didn't, judging from Paul's expression.

She replaced the urn in the glass case, locked it, then handed the key to Paul. "I'm sorry. That wasn't kind. I know that church business is confidential . . . It's just that—"

He interrupted her. "Actually, it wasn't church business."

But he didn't offer any further explanation. He gestured toward the urn. "Did you discover anything new?"

"Only that I'm even more puzzled by the language on the base. I'd like to have someone translate it, but such a person might be hard to find in Copper Mill."

"Didn't Renee say something about Collin translating it?"

"She did, but it wasn't anything definitive."

Actually, nothing Kate had heard about Collin Wellington seemed definitive. But she couldn't pinpoint exactly what it was that bothered her about him. Shouldn't it be enough that Renee and the others on the tour seemed to trust him?

She held at bay the *no* that slammed into her mind and

concentrated instead on her husband's mysterious telephone calls.

Paul held the outer door open, and she stepped out into the bright morning sunlight. He followed and walked her to the Honda.

"I thought I'd drop by the library and see if I can find something online about the language origins."

He opened the driver's side door, and she slid in. "You do know how much I love you, don't you?" He gazed into her eyes.

She blinked. He often told her he loved her, but this felt out of the blue.

"Well, yes, I do, but—"

He stooped and gave her a quick kiss. "Then you need to trust me." He squeezed her arm affectionately before heading back toward the church entrance. He trotted up the steps, then turned and waved as she drove off.

TWO HOURS LATER, Kate and Livvy settled into a blue vinyl booth at the Country Diner.

"I tell you, Livvy, I'm worried about Paul. He's keeping something from me, and it may be serious." She was surprised when her eyes welled with tears. "The only thing I can figure is that it might be his health. He went in for a checkup last week, and maybe it was bad news that he doesn't want me to worry about."

Livvy blinked, a little nervously, it seemed to Kate, then recovered quickly and patted Kate's hand. Kate wondered if she was getting paranoid. She was beginning to think everyone close to her was in on something, but she had no idea what.

Now with nothing but concern in her expression, Livvy said gently, "Something tells me that's not all you're worried about."

Kate gave her a shaky smile and told her friend about Melissa's call and the alarm and sadness she detected in her voice. She pulled a tissue from her handbag. "Listen to me, I sound like the bearer of bad news. So far, this conversation has been only about my concerns."

"That's what friends are for," Livvy said. "And now I know how I can pray for you."

LuAnne stepped up with her pad and pencil at the ready. "*Buon giorno*, girls, what'll it be? The *capricciosa* for today is some awfully good chicken potpies fresh out of the oven. Local-grown carrots and free-range chicken, if you care about such things. Gravy thick as molasses in a hailstorm. Crust that'll make you think of your grandma's." She kissed her fingertips Italian style. "Best part, there's not a calorie in the whole thing." She chuckled and winked.

Kate and Livvy agreed that it sounded good and ordered one to split, and iced tea.

After LuAnne left with their order, Kate leaned forward. "*Capricciosa?*"

Livvy laughed. "It's either 'chef's choice' or 'baby goat.' I forget."

Kate laughed. "Speaking of Italy, Paul and I read your article this morning and loved it. It made me feel as if I were right there with you. I bet all the *Chronicle* readers feel the same way."

Livvy looked pleased. "Thanks. Renee and Collin's budding romance was such a delight to us all. I couldn't help writing about it."

LuAnne returned with their iced teas, then headed to another table to take an order.

"Knowing Renee," Kate said after a sip of tea, "I'm sure she was delighted to be featured in the story."

Livvy laughed. "Delighted is an understatement. Actually, she came up with the idea of me writing a column about the trip and hinted strongly that I should feature the story of her and Collin falling in love in such a romantic place."

Kate chuckled with her. "That's our Renee."

Livvy nodded. "And, it seems, also our Collin?"

"He agreed to their story being told?"

"More than that. Renee told me that he'd been the one to put the bug in her ear, about asking me to write the articles." She paused and took a sip of tea. "He was also the one who insisted we take the photo that was in the paper this morning. He said he wanted to remember standing beside Renee at the Neptune Fountain for the rest of his life."

"It must have been love at first sight," Kate said, again attempting to keep her niggling doubts about Collin at bay. "Who would have thought such a thing could happen so quickly to Renee?"

LuAnne brought their chicken potpie, with an extra plate and serving spoon. As Kate cut across the pie, the fragrance of chicken and rosemary made her and Livvy sigh. She scooped half onto the extra plate and handed it to Livvy, who closed her eyes and inhaled, looking as if she'd just received manna from heaven.

As they ate, Kate told Livvy about stopping by the church to have another look at the urn, and about the beauty of the display.

"It's a unique piece of art, no doubt about it," Livvy said, her fork hovering over a piece of golden crust.

"Did you get a close enough look to see the hairline fractures?" Kate took a sip of iced tea and dabbed at her mouth with the corner of her napkin.

Livvy's brow furrowed in thought. "I did take a pretty good look right after Renee bought it. All of us did. But I didn't notice anything unusual. The only thing I found odd is that there is some ancient code for opening it." She laughed. "The first time Collin opened it, he obviously wanted to prove to Renee that there were no ashes inside. A few of the others of us tried the formula, and bingo, it opened. It was rather complicated, but we did it."

She shook her head slowly, smiling at the memory. "Collin said it was unique in that it's an incredibly well-done copy of the original."

"Does anyone know where the original is located?"

Livvy looked thoughtful. "*Hmm.* That never came up. I couldn't tell you."

They ate for a few more minutes in silence, then Livvy took a sip of tea and sat back. "Wait a minute. You're onto something, aren't you?"

Kate laughed. "Maybe, I guess. I was just struck by the beauty of the urn and what a magnificent replica it is." She grinned. In fact, it was such a stunning piece that Kate had the idea that it may not be a replica at all.

However, despite the fact that Livvy was her best friend, Kate wasn't quite ready to tell her about the doubts that kept popping into her mind. Doubts that made her wonder if the piece might be an original.

Livvy studied Kate for a moment as if she knew Kate was holding something back. "Well, at any rate, it seems you're not the only one in these parts who's interested. I received an e-mail this morning from a Dr. Hosea inquiring about the urn." She lifted her brow as if in a friendly challenge.

Kate grinned and took the bait. "Who's Dr. Hosea?"

"An archaeologist who lives in southern Tennessee, and a world-renowned expert in ancient artifacts. I Googled his name to check his credentials. He's a well-known author and highly respected, from what I gathered."

"How did he happen to contact you?"

Livvy shook her head. "He contacted the *Chronicle's* office after reading their online version of the paper. They forwarded his e-mail to me."

"Very interesting," Kate said, sipping her tea. "Especially since this supposedly is a replica. Would you mind if I contacted him?"

"Not at all," Livvy said. "You know as much about the urn as I do."

A HALF HOUR LATER, Kate was seated at the bank of computers on the second floor of the library. After logging in to her personal e-mail account, she began composing a note to Dr. Hosea. She described the urn in great detail, including her observations about the hairline cracks in the alabaster.

She reread the post, then clicked Send. Four other e-mails were listed in her in-box—two from friends in San Antonio; one from her son, Andrew; and one an advertisement for a new computer. She answered the first three, dumped the fourth, then aimed the cursor to the computer's desktop menu to log off.

Just then, she received notice that she had a new e-mail.

Curious, she opened the program again. Dr. Hosea's reply was listed in her mailbox. Surprised that he'd gotten back to her so quickly, she clicked on the e-mail to open it. Her eyes widened as she read: "You may have an extremely important find. Send photos immediately, if you have them."

Chapter Five

The ringing telephone jarred Kate awake. She looked at the bedside clock: 5:23 AM. Her first thought was that it had to be Renee, who was obviously still fighting jet lag. Stifling a groan, she rubbed her eyes and swung her feet over the side of the bed.

Then it hit her.

Melissa!

She grabbed her robe and, not bothering with her slippers, picked up the cordless receiver on the third ring. She headed as fast as she could toward the kitchen so she wouldn't wake Paul.

"Mom . . . ?"

"Yes, honey. I'm here."

"I'm sorry to call so early, but I know you're an early riser. I didn't think you'd mind. Besides, I just needed to hear your voice right now."

Kate fell into a nearby chair. "We've been waiting for your call—and praying for you every minute."

Melissa didn't answer right away. "Thank you," she said, her voice barely audible. "Our appointments are set up, John finished his project, and we're leaving tomorrow morning. I can't wait to get there, to see you and Daddy." Her voice trembled, and she cleared her throat.

Kate took a deep breath. "You'll be here early. That's good. By noon, do you think?"

"We . . . ah . . . well, not that early. We have some business to take care of on our way."

"Business?"

The moment of silence that followed threatened to break Kate's heart. "Honey, we already suspect something awful has happened. The reality can't be any worse than what we're imagining. I want to honor your wishes to wait till you get here to tell us what it is, but I must also let you know how much we wish you would tell us what's going on."

She hesitated as she heard Melissa's soft sniffles on the other end of the line. "Sweetie, wouldn't it help you and John somehow lessen the burden you two are carrying to know we're in this with you?"

Melissa blew her nose. "Mom, I've wanted to tell you, I have from the beginning. Maybe now is the right time, at least so you know in general what we're dealing with." She started to cry softly. "It's just so hard . . ."

"I'm here, sweetie." Kate's heart was racing.

Just then, Mia's wail and Melissa's quick intake of breath made Kate's knees turn to jelly. "Melissa—"

Melissa put down the phone with a clatter, and Kate could hear her soft comforting murmurs, the tiny sobs gradually quieting, and then her daughter returned to the phone.

"Mia fell and bumped her head," she said. "Nothing serious . . ."

Kate smiled, remembering those bumps and wails she'd dealt with when the kids were toddlers. The cuddles and kissing the boo-boos afterward, the ceremonial Band-Aids. When Melissa was a two-year-old, she thought Band-Aids made all boo-boos go away, even headaches.

"You were about to tell me what's happened," she said softly.

"I can't now," Melissa said, and Kate pictured her daughter's cheek resting on Mia's head, the baby's arms wrapped around Melissa's neck. "Not with Mia here."

Not with Mia here?

"But we'll see you tomorrow, probably early afternoon." Melissa's voice seemed unnaturally cheerful.

"We can't wait to see you, honey," Kate said. "Please drive carefully."

"We will . . . and Mama . . ."

"Yes?"

"Thank you for, well, for being you." She sniffled again. "I can't wait to be safe in your arms."

Kate blinked back the quick tears that stung her eyes as she pictured her daughter as a toddler again, coming to her to kiss away the boo-boo. Oh, that life were that simple now.

As soon as they said their good-byes, Kate bowed her head and prayed again for Melissa, John, and Mia. She leaned against the counter for strength. It was something troubling, she knew. But what? Marital problems? Health issues? John's job? Financial issues?

IT WAS GETTING CLOSE to six thirty when, after finishing her morning prayers, Kate got up from her rocker and went back into the kitchen.

Outdoors, the morning had dawned balmy and bright. Kate hummed "His Eye Is on the Sparrow" as she poured a second cup of coffee for herself and a first cup for Paul, who had just rounded the corner into the kitchen.

"Cinnamon rolls," he announced. "I'd recognize that scent anywhere." He chuckled as he headed to the table and sat down where Kate had placed his mug. Even though he was trying to remain upbeat, probably for her sake, Kate could see in his expression that he must have overheard Melissa's call.

"It's a new recipe made with quick-rise dough." She snapped her fingers. "Takes no longer than three shakes of a Javalina's tail."

He grinned. "Javalina's tail?"

"I'm from Texas, remember?" Then she sobered. "The kids will be here tomorrow." She slipped into the chair across the table from him. "When Melissa called, she said they were getting ready to leave."

Paul's forehead furrowed with worry. "I've gone over what could be wrong a thousand times."

"I have too," Kate said, giving him a soft smile. "And as we've told each other a thousand times, we need to leave it in God's hands." She reached for her mug. "I had an idea this morning while I was stirring together the ingredients."

"About the kids?"

"Well, specifically about Melissa. She sounded so stressed

this morning that I thought it might be nice to do something special for her."

"I agree. What do you have in mind?"

"I've gone through a list of possibilities, but I keep coming back to choosing something for her that she would never choose for herself."

Paul sipped his coffee, then a corner of his mouth twitched into a half smile. "Why do I think it's probably a girl thing?"

The timer chimed, and Kate stood and headed to the stove. "Very perceptive." Stooping to peer into the oven, she turned and gave him a quick grin, then pulled out the pan of rolls.

"While you tell me about it, why don't I help you with a taste test." He waggled his eyebrows.

"I wouldn't have it any other way." She scooped two buns from the pan and placed the larger one on a plate for Paul, the smaller on her own plate, then grabbed two forks from the flatware drawer.

Paul refreshed their coffee and sat down again across from her. They bowed their heads, and after saying an earnest prayer for their children, Paul thanked God for his abundant provision.

"Tell me," he said after he'd taken his first bite of cinnamon roll, "what do you have in mind for Melissa?"

"A spa treatment. Maybe a manicure or pedicure, or even a massage if you think we can afford it." Kate watched for his reaction. Since he'd told her that they couldn't manage the Italy trip because finances were tight, she had been even more careful than usual about her spending habits, even on gifts for others.

"I think that's a splendid idea," Paul said. "I would like to heap some TLC on them while they're here. Maybe I can come up with something for John . . . He mentioned a book last time we were together—a Grisham novel, I think."

They cleared the table and took the dishes to the sink, talking about gift ideas for Mia. Kate said she needed to drop by the Mercantile later anyway for groceries, and she would look for something in the toy section.

As she pulled a piece of cellophane wrap over the rolls, she added, "I'll stop by the bank too. I'll move some money from savings to take care of all this."

For a moment Paul didn't speak. Then he said, "You've got enough to do, getting ready for the kids coming and all. I can easily stop at the bank, save you the trouble."

"Oh, it's no trouble at all. I'll do it." Was it her imagination or did he look suddenly worried about something?

"Paul," she said, resting her hand on his forearm. "If there's some reason we shouldn't spend the money right now, please tell me."

He shrugged. "There's no reason," he said. "I just wanted to save you a few steps in your busy day."

WHEN KATE HAD FINISHED her shopping at the Mercantile, she stopped at Mid-Cumberland Bank and Trust on her way to the spa at the Hamilton Springs Hotel.

She filled out a transfer slip, then headed to Georgia Cline's teller station and handed her the paper.

Georgia took it with a smile, typed the account information into her computer, then made the transaction. As soon as it was complete, she handed Kate a printout of both accounts.

Kate had taken a few steps away from Georgia's window

when she glanced at the balance in the savings account. She studied it a moment, then turned back.

"Georgia, I think there must be some mistake," she said. "My last statement showed a balance with significantly more money in savings."

Georgia patted her hair, adjusted her reading glasses, then tapped away at her keyboard. She turned the screen toward Kate to show her the individual transactions on the account.

"A three-thousand-dollar withdrawal," Kate breathed. "That's got to be an error. We haven't taken that much money out."

"Your husband is the one who authorized the transaction," Georgia said. "Maybe he forgot to mention it."

Kate felt the blood drain out of her face. "You're sure there hasn't been an error?"

Georgia gave her a worried smile. "I can show you his signature if you'd care to wait."

Kate stared at her for a moment, then shook her head. "No, no. That won't be necessary. Thank you."

With a heavy heart, she walked back outside to her car. For a moment, she rested her forehead against the steering wheel. Why would Paul withdraw so much money without telling her? The only reason she could think of was that they were in more serious financial trouble than he'd let on. Though he kept track of their accounts, she had a pretty good handle on their balances too.

And this withdrawal was shocking. Was he trying to protect her? And from what? Again, concerns about his health stabbed at her heart.

A few minutes later, she drove the Honda into the garage and parked. Paul looked up from where he was tinkering with something at his workbench. He gave her a big smile as she stepped out of the car.

"Did you get everything you needed?"

She shook her head numbly. "Not everything. I . . . I . . . I stopped by the bank to transfer the money to checking . . ." Her words faltered as she searched his eyes. "When I found out that there wasn't as much as I thought, I decided against getting the gift for Melissa."

He came over to her and put his hands on her shoulders. Before she could say anything more, he placed his index finger over her lips.

"I'll say it again. I need you to trust me, Kate."

She reached for his hand and gently squeezed his fingers. "Of course I do."

"In every regard."

She let out a pent-up sigh as she studied the love in his gaze. Finally, she nodded. "All right. I'll trust you to tell me what's going on in good time."

"In good time," he repeated, then went to the back of the car to carry in her bags of groceries.

Chapter Six

Early the next morning, as soon as Kate had finished her morning devotions, she padded to Paul's study and sat down in front of the computer. The parsonage didn't have access to a high-speed connection, so researching anything on the Internet was painfully slow. Even so, she could check her e-mail, and she was eager to see if she'd heard anything more from Dr. Hosea.

She turned on the machine and waited patiently while the programs loaded. Finally, her e-mail program came up, and she clicked on her in-box, then the first post on her list. The subject line simply read: Photos?

"I am eagerly awaiting your photos of the urn," Dr. Hosea wrote, "particularly close-ups. Please understand the importance of this."

Kate wasn't surprised by the urgent tone of the note. It somehow confirmed her own growing suspicions. She sent a reply that said she would send the photos as soon as she could, then she sat back to think about this response.

What if this urn was the real thing? What would that mean for Renee? How might it relate to Kate's growing doubts about Collin?

After logging out of her e-mail account, she headed to the kitchen for a coffee refill and to plan for the busy day ahead. She wanted to make a batch of ginger cookies in circus-animal shapes for Mia. She wondered if she'd ever baked this many batches of cookies for anything other than a church potluck. No doubt, she loved to bake while puzzling a mystery, but this was different. Fixing meals for others, especially baking something special for those she loved, was a tangible way for her to demonstrate her affection.

She had just started to cream the butter and sugar when the phone rang. Flipping off the switch on her mixer, she grabbed for the phone and picked it up on the second ring.

It was Renee. "I just got another letter from Collin. And oh, my dear, I *must* read it to you."

Without waiting for Kate to respond, she began to read:

"My darling Lady Renee,

> How I miss you. Though it's only been days, it feels like weeks since we last saw each other. I cannot believe how destiny brought us together. I wish I were a poet, but even then words could not convey the deep emotions that fill my heart . . . and my soul . . ."

Renee went on to read the rest of the letter, which grew increasingly flowery, yet with a British flavor.

"Lady Renee?" Kate couldn't help asking at the end.

Renee chuckled. "A private joke." Then her voice dropped. "I haven't felt so, well, cherished for a very long time. A very long time." Her words were dramatic, but her emotion was genuine.

What if Collin was out to hurt Renee? Kate didn't want to go that far with her suspicions, so she quickly pushed the thought aside.

Paul came around the corner into the kitchen. He gave Kate a peck on the cheek, then poured his coffee and sat down at the table.

She said good-bye to Renee and sat down across from him.

She told Paul about the latest e-mail from Dr. Hosea and her need to run by the church and take pictures.

"I'll go with you, if it will help."

She gave him a soft smile. "I'd love nothing better."

Keeping busy until the kids arrived was the best anti-worry antidote she could think of for them both.

That and prayer.

IT WAS LATE MORNING when Kate headed into the library to upload the photos of the urn from her camera onto the computer.

She had left Paul at Faith Briar to put the finishing touches on his sermon and promised she would meet him at home for lunch. Time was of the essence. She glanced at her watch. She had barely fifteen minutes to complete the upload and send the photographs to Dr. Hosea.

After a few minutes, the pictures of the urn began to appear on the computer, lined up, looking professional. She grinned. Phase one complete.

She glanced down at her watch. Nine minutes left before she had to leave to meet Paul. She wrote a quick message to Dr. Hosea, typed in his address, then began attaching the photos from the camera file.

One by one they attached themselves to the e-mail. She soon had a dozen in place, and the e-mail was obviously ready to make its way through cyberspace. She clicked Send.

She sat back in her chair, closed her eyes, breathed deeply, then opened her eyes again. She spent her last few minutes answering other e-mails, then reached for the mouse to log out of her e-mail account.

Her breath caught in her throat when she saw that a return e-mail had already landed in her in-box.

Dear Mrs. Hanlon,

After a cursory glance at the photos you sent, I am even more intrigued by the urn. The cracked and pitted surface shows patterns of aging particular to centuries-old alabaster. These are very difficult to duplicate, and costly, because most souvenir-grade copies are made of a resin-type material. I would like to examine the urn in person and perhaps run further tests to determine its authenticity. If my suspicions are correct, we may be dealing with an original artifact with a greater value than can be imagined.

Kate quickly reread the note to make sure she'd gotten it right.

An original artifact?

When she could breathe again, she noticed his postscript: "Please telephone my office as soon as you can."

She made note of the phone number, then folded the paper and tucked it into her handbag.

She trotted down the stairs, waved at Livvy, then exited the library, heading for her car.

Once inside, she clutched the steering wheel, stunned at the turn of events.

An original artifact? The words played over and over in her mind.

She turned the key in the ignition, then sat back, nibbling at her bottom lip. As she backed out of her parking place, a thought suddenly occurred to her. Why hadn't Dr. Hosea mentioned the faded inscription around the bottom?

With his expertise, he must be able to read it. One would think that would be of utmost importance. But then, he had written his response so quickly and urgently, he probably hadn't had time to give the photos a proper inspection.

KATE AND PAUL had just finished lunch when John and Melissa's car pulled up to the parsonage. They hurried to the front door and flung it open even before the kids were out of the car.

Melissa ran into her mother's open arms. John came up the walkway behind her, a sleepy-looking Mia in his arms. When Melissa pulled back, Kate could see her eyes were swollen and red. Kate noticed that they filled when she hugged her father.

Even though Mia was snuggling against her father's shoulder, there was something about her that seemed different.

Gone were the rosy cheeks, the big smile that showed all

her teeth, the squealing giggles she usually had the instant her grandma came into sight.

Instead, she just fixed her gaze first on Kate, then on Paul, with her big blue eyes, and then lay still. Her arms were thinner too, and her tiny face seemed pinched and thin.

Then it hit her, and Kate almost gasped.

Was something wrong with Mia? Was that why they'd come?

Chapter Seven

As they moved into the living room, Paul and Kate exchanged glances, and Paul reached for her hand. They had agreed beforehand to let John and Melissa take the lead, but Kate found it difficult to wait, now that they were here. Now that she suspected Mia was at the center of their concerns.

John stood slightly behind Melissa, attempting to smile, but his expression said something was terribly wrong. Mia was perched on his arm, and he had curled his other arm protectively around her.

"We need to put Mia down for a nap," John said quietly. "She's had a tiring day."

Melissa stepped nearer to her husband and combed back strands of the toddler's blonde hair with her fingertips. Mia looked up at her mother and gave her a wan smile. Kate loved that her granddaughter had inherited Paul's vivid blue eyes that sparkled with life.

Melissa's hair was much like Kate's—strawberry blonde, though more reddish—and she wore it in a chin-length bob, which accentuated her heart-shaped face. She had always been petite, and now she seemed thinner than ever, her eyes reflecting some sort of inner sorrow.

Kate went over to stand beside them, and Paul did the same, circling his arm around Kate.

"Our little angel . . . ," Kate whispered and brushed the backs of her fingers against Mia's soft cheek.

"We'll get her settled," John said. "And then we'll tell you everything . . . about our little angel."

Kate's heart dropped. She glanced at Paul, whose face had turned ashen.

John and Melissa took the baby into Paul's study where Paul had already set up a borrowed port-a-crib. When they returned to the living room, the couple sat close together on the sofa.

Paul settled into a chair, but Kate stood by the rocker. "Would either of you like a soft drink or some iced tea?"

After their long drive, she thought they might be thirsty. Besides, from the look of things, what the kids were about to tell them wouldn't be easy. A cool drink might help them get through it.

"Sounds wonderful. Let me help you, Mom," Melissa said.

She stood and accompanied her mother to the kitchen. An awkward silence fell between mother and daughter. Kate so desperately wanted to take Melissa in her arms and comfort her, but Melissa clearly wasn't ready to talk.

After a few minutes, they returned with their drinks. Kate set a plate of cookies on the coffee table. John gave her a grateful smile, but he didn't reach for one.

Paul was the first to speak. "We've been praying for you.

Your mother and I both sensed that something must be terribly wrong or you would have told us on the phone."

John glanced at Melissa. "Do you want me to start?"

She nodded, and he circled his arm around her shoulders.

"It's about Mia," he said. "About three months ago, we started noticing some changes in Mia. The first sign was her weight. She just didn't seem to be gaining the weight she should for her age and height."

"I remember you telling us about her weight," Kate said to Melissa. "But you were a slender toddler too, so I attributed it to that."

"That's what we thought," John said. "It wasn't until a week ago that it was obvious something else was wrong."

Kate exchanged a quick glance with her daughter. From her expression, Melissa obviously knew what she was thinking. "We didn't want to worry you or Dad until we knew more," she said gently. "This came on so fast, and our focus has been on Mia . . . and setting up her appointments with the specialist."

Melissa glanced at John, who then went on. "The doctor had already been monitoring her weight, but when she began to have difficulty breathing last week, he started looking elsewhere for the cause. At first he thought it might be asthma."

Melissa sat forward, her gaze intense. "It made sense that maybe the onset of asthma might cause her to lose interest in food. But her pediatrician wanted to run further tests, and we agreed."

She blinked back fresh tears and tucked a strand of hair behind one ear, a habit carried over from childhood. "Then a few days ago, after her nap, Mia tried to pull herself up to stand in her crib. I came into her room just as she toppled backward. At first I thought she'd stopped breathing, but when I picked her up . . ." Melissa started to cry quietly.

John took her hand and continued. "I was in the kitchen, and when Melissa called for me, I came running. I called 911, and the EMTs got there within minutes. By the time they did, Mia had opened her eyes and was smiling up at us and looking around as if to say, 'What's all the fuss about?'"

"The doctor immediately ran more tests, this time focusing on her heart," Melissa said, her voice still trembling. She sipped her iced tea, then drew in a deep breath. "When the results came back, he recommended that we bring Mia to Tennessee to see a friend of his from med school."

John had again wrapped his arm around Melissa's shoulders. She looked up at him as if for strength, as he said, "He's a pediatric specialist in congenital heart defects."

Congenital heart defects? Kate felt the sting of tears at the back of her throat and reached for her iced tea as a distraction. She needed to be strong for Melissa and John. She heard Paul clear his throat, then he reached for his drink, a sure sign that he was in the middle of his own emotional battle.

"The specialist, Dr. Timothy Lucas, practices in Pine Ridge," Melissa said. "As soon as we found that out, we decided there's no place we'd rather be than here with you."

John broke in. "He was born and raised in Pine Ridge, and after he finished his internship and residency, felt led to return to his hometown. He had his pick of university hospitals and big city medical centers to choose from, but he chose to come home and treat the babies and children who need him the most."

"We think that says a lot about his character," Melissa added.

Kate finally trusted her voice enough to speak. "What treatments are being considered? Did your pediatrician give you any indication?"

Melissa took a deep breath. "We won't know, of course, until more tests are run, but it could be anything from medication to open-heart surgery."

When Kate heard the word *surgery*, another sting at the top of her throat told her a flood of tears was on its way if she didn't do something fast. She needed to be strong for her daughter and John, for them all. She blinked rapidly, sipped her tea again, and then reached for the plate of cookies, offering it around. This time John took one, and so did Paul, but Melissa shook her head.

John popped the cookie into his mouth and chewed thoughtfully for a moment. Then he said, "Dr. Lucas is considered to be an excellent doctor. He's part of a team of specialists that often travel to medical schools here and in other countries to work with other pediatricians on new diagnostic techniques. From everything we've heard about him, we feel that he—and maybe others in his team—can give us the best advice and diagnosis for Mia. That is the great blessing in all this. Our little daughter will be in good hands."

Melissa gave her mom and dad a tremulous smile. "The other blessing is that we can be here with you, knowing you'll hold us up in prayer, moment by moment."

"We're so glad you've come," Paul said quietly. "You know you're welcome anytime, but now especially, you need to know that our home is yours. And anything we can do to help, we'll be available day or night."

Melissa went over to give her dad a hug. Paul stood and drew his daughter into his arms. Kate did the same, wrapping her arms around them both.

"I feel better just being here with you," Melissa whispered.

John was now standing beside her. He took her hand, his expression somber. "Dad, would you offer a prayer for Mia?"

Paul nodded. "Let's go in and stand by her crib."

John's eyes glistened with tears. "Thank you."

Moments later, the four adults circled the little port-a-crib, holding hands.

"Father," Paul prayed, his voice a low whisper, "sometimes it is so hard to find the words to express the heaviness in our hearts—and even to know how to pray. But you know our hearts better than we do ourselves. And you know Mia's needs right now. Cradle her in your arms, heavenly Father. Give her the tender care that only you can provide. And give us, her parents and grandparents, your peace that passes all understanding with the assurance that you are with all of us each step of the way."

He paused, and everyone joined him to breathe a soft amen.

At the sound of their voices, Mia woke. She blinked at the faces looking down at her, rubbed her eyes, then sat up. When she saw Kate, she gave her a big smile and held out her arms to be picked up.

One glance at Melissa's face told Kate Mia hadn't slept as long as they'd hoped.

"Why don't you try rocking her back to sleep," she whispered to Kate.

As Kate drew her granddaughter into her arms, she held her close, never wanting to let go.

Chapter Eight

Early Monday morning, John and Melissa bundled Mia into the car, buckled her into her car seat, and left for Pine Ridge and their first appointment with Dr. Lucas.

"I would give anything to bear this burden for them," Kate said as she and Paul waved them off.

They turned and went back into the house, then headed for the kitchen to clean up the breakfast dishes.

"I feel the same way," Paul said.

He picked up the plates from the table, carried them to the sink, and started to rinse off the remaining pancake crumbs and sticky syrup. "But a wise man once told me that the best way to bear another's burden is to listen with your heart to the one who is hurting and to let them know you care." He turned around to face Kate, looking thoughtful. "He also had some wise thoughts about binding up the brokenhearted."

Kate nodded as she stooped to clean up the blue pancake crumbs beneath the high chair; it was the color Mia had chosen when she helped Kate mix the batter earlier.

"And we're certainly doing that," she said when she stood. "I just wish we could be with them every step of the way." She moved to the counter and, after tearing off a fresh paper towel from the roll, wiped up the blue batter spills around her mixer. "Something tells me that wise man is Nehemiah."

Paul's grin widened. "How'd you guess?"

Nehemiah Jacobs was Paul's mentor. Paul had known him since childhood, and it was Nehemiah's preaching that led Paul to become a minister. Nehemiah had retired as pastor of Faith Briar and was now living in a retirement facility, but Paul still visited with him as often as he could.

Kate laughed softly. "Because you quote Nehemiah more than most anyone else when it comes to things of the Spirit. Especially when it involves ministering to others."

"At his age, he's had a lot of life experience. Not to mention the time he's spent on his knees. A few minutes in his presence, listening to his words of wisdom, says more to my heart than reading a half dozen how-to tomes on pastoral care."

"You were about to tell me something he said about binding up the brokenhearted."

Paul leaned back against the counter. He'd tossed a dishtowel over his shoulder Emeril Lagasse-style.

"He said that as much as we might want to carry the full burden of heartache for those we love, we can't. It's something they must face head-on. They can't go over it or under it or around it. They must go through the circumstance themselves."

Kate drew in a thoughtful breath. "Our role, then, is to love them through it." She paused long enough to toss the paper towel in the wastebasket under the sink. "That's hard. I'm a fixer, especially when it comes to our children."

"You've always been wonderfully hands-on," Paul agreed. "But as our kids grow older, they don't need us in the same way."

"That's difficult to get used to. Just when I think I'm over the empty-nest thing, it crops up again. I'd like to step out with a big *ta-da!* and drumroll announcing that Mom's coming to the rescue." She went over to stand close to Paul, and he drew her into his arms.

"Only this time you—*we*—can't," he said quietly, resting his cheek on top of her head.

"And that's what hurts so much."

AFTER PAUL LEFT for coffee at the diner with the other pastors in town, Kate picked up the phone to call Dr. Hosea. He'd apparently given her his office number, and all she got was a recording that said he was out of the office for the day.

She started to leave a voice-mail message, then decided he might get in touch with her sooner through e-mail. Disappointed she hadn't been able to reach him, she ran through her options in her mind. No matter what she would learn from Dr. Hosea, her own curiosity compelled her to do a little more digging.

At the top of the list of options, which included baking a batch of cranberry-pecan cookies to help her think things through, was another trip to the library to do research. She could always bake cookies afterward, and maybe she would have more information to mull over in the process.

KATE HAD JUST PULLED the Honda into the library parking spot by the wild-rose vine, when Caroline Beauregard Johnston marched toward her car, waving her cane.

Renee's mother might have been in her nineties, but she was a spitfire. Kate, and everyone else in town, knew exactly where Renee got her outspoken spunk and propensity for drama.

Kate got out of the car and gave the older woman a wide smile. "Well, hello, Caroline. You're out early on a beautiful morn—"

"Beautiful morning, my foot," she said, moving closer. The froth of silk flowers atop her straw hat fluttered with each step. "Other people might see it that way, but I certainly don't."

"I'm sorry to hear—"

"Not half as sorry as I am. I suppose you've heard the news?"

Kate silently ran through the short list of possibilities, then settled on the obvious. "You mean about Renee and Collin?"

"What else?" Caroline sputtered. "Carrying on like a teenager with that new beau of hers. You should hear them on the phone. It's embarrassing, that's what it is."

"She told me that he's quite a gentleman. She said he's intelligent, well read, interesting to be with, and he can make a decent cup of English tea."

"Fiddle-faddle. I don't care who he says he is. I say he's a gold digger. Out to get my daughter's money." She stepped closer. "He's a younger man, you know. He wants to marry Renee so he won't have to work another day in his life."

"Isn't he already retir—"

"I know the type," she said. "He probably wants to be remembered in her will. Mine too, if truth be known."

"Maybe when you meet him in person, you'll change your mind. Even Livvy says he's very nice and treated Renee like a queen."

"*Hmmph.* They all do at first." Caroline tapped her cane on the pavement for emphasis. "Mark my words, no earthly good can come of this. Nothing you or anyone else can say will convince me otherwise."

Before Kate could respond, she said, "Now, if you'll excuse me. I have friends waiting for me at the Mercantile."

"Would you like for me to drive you?"

Caroline let out another *hmmph.* "Do I look like I need help across the street? I think not." She walked away, the flowers on her straw hat bobbing with each step and tap of the cane.

I'd rather be spunky when I'm her age, Kate thought with a grin, *than to sit in my rocker and let the world go by without me.* She was still chuckling to herself as she entered the library.

A few minutes later, she took her seat at the bank of computers. She put in her password, opened her e-mail program, and clicked on the photos she had sent to Dr. Hosea. Next, she enlarged the one with the close-up of the symbols that were vaguely familiar to her.

She kept it visible on one side of the computer screen while she did a search for ancient languages. She clicked through several Web sites, then one stood out.

Etruscan.

Of course, that's why the symbols had looked familiar. When she studied ancient history in college, one entire semester was spent on early Italian history, which included a look at the influence of the Etruscan people on the Roman civilization that came after them.

She stared at the symbols and letters of the ancient

language, then compared them with those on the urn. It was a match, not symbol for symbol, but enough of a similarity to know she was right: the inscription was Etruscan.

She sat back, crossed her arms, and stared at the photo of the urn on her screen. Why would the person who designed the urn, whether it was an original or a copy, pair a twelfth-century design with a language that preceded it by more than a thousand years?

Kate clicked the mouse to pull up another photograph, this time of the relief images of St. Francis and Clare. There was something very tender in their faces, and as she enlarged the photo, she noticed that the artist had captured an expression that spoke of a love that went far beyond the romantic, or even sentimental.

There was a beauty to the piece that made her believe its value was more than that of a run-of-the-mill souvenir. Maybe that was why she couldn't give up getting to the bottom of its origin.

Maybe there wasn't any more mystery to the piece than that: it held a luminous beauty all its own, and Collin Wellington chose it for Renee for that reason. Though she did wonder if he, an expert on such antiquities, might have noticed the language curiosity. And what about Dr. Hosea? Had he noticed?

She chided herself for her circular thinking and started to log off the computer. Then on a whim, she stopped, pulled up Google, and typed in Collin's name. A number of Web pages came up, including links to scholarly papers he'd published, announcements of past speaking engagements, even an announcement of a recent audience with Queen Elizabeth. Most prominently displayed was the Oxford University Web site, where his curriculum vitae was listed with that of other retired faculty.

She smiled to herself as she noted his age. Caroline was right; he was younger than Renee. All of two years younger.

AS KATE WALKED toward her car a few minutes later, Renee's pink Oldsmobile pulled out of the alley behind the Mercantile where she'd picked up Caroline. She turned right toward Sweetwater, but when she saw Kate, she threw her boat of a car into reverse. Without looking, she backed up, then screeched to a halt beside Kate's Honda.

Before Kate could say hello, Renee had leaped from the car, waving an envelope. The radiance of her smile made her look three decades younger than her seventy-something years.

"It's from Collin," she said. "He's coming for a visit!"

"That's wonderful," Kate said, and meant it. She thought of all the questions she had about the urn. "I really can't wait to meet him."

Renee stepped closer and added dramatically, "I think he's planning to pop the question."

A loud *hmmph* erupted from the passenger side of the Oldsmobile, then Caroline rolled up the window and sat staring dead ahead, her lips drawn in a tight line.

"Poor Mama," Renee said, surprising Kate with her touch of sympathy. "She's worried I'll say yes."

Kate tilted her head. "And will you?"

The breeze ruffled the leaves of the wild roses behind them, and as the scent of roses filled the air, Renee sighed.

On a whim, Kate reached over and picked a clump of the pale pink roses on a single stem and handed it to Renee.

For a moment neither woman spoke. When Renee's eyes met Kate's, they were watery.

"That's illegal, you know," she said with a sniff. Then with a small nod and an expression that gave Kate a brief glimpse into her heart, Renee fluttered her manicured fingers and slid beneath the steering wheel of the big pink vehicle.

"Change can be good, Mama," Kate thought she heard Renee say as they drove off.

Though she couldn't hear it, she knew what Caroline's response would be.

Chapter Nine

When the kids arrived home from their doctor's trip to Pine Ridge, Kate and Melissa spread a quilt on the grass beneath the maple tree. Mia was still sleepy from her nap in the car and seemed content to cuddle in Kate's lap.

Kate had put together a meat loaf and popped it into the oven, along with four baked potatoes, a half hour earlier. Already, the savory scent wafted through the sliding screen door.

Melissa leaned back, propping herself with her arms, her legs straight out in front of her, one ankle hooked over the other. She filled Kate in on the details of their first appointment with Dr. Lucas. She and John had both liked Dr. Lucas from the moment they met, especially his playful and gentle demeanor with Mia.

"But until he runs the tests and we get the results back, we won't know anything more than we do now."

"How are you doing—emotionally, I mean—with all this uncertainty?" Kate shifted Mia so the toddler was resting in the crook of her arm.

Melissa reached for her mother's hand. "As long as I stay focused on Mia, I'm okay. The Lord loves her more than John or I ever could. But if I start worrying about our tomorrows, her tomorrows, I get pretty scared."

"It's okay to be scared," Kate said.

Melissa's eyes filled. "I try to be strong for John's sake, and, of course, for Mia, but sometimes I feel overwhelmed, like the burden is too much to carry."

Kate squeezed her daughter's fingers and then released them when Melissa reached for a tissue. "In Isaiah we're told the Lord God himself will wipe away the tears from the faces of his people. That leads me to believe that our tears are precious to him, and that it's okay to cry."

Melissa let out a deep pent-up breath and leaned back on the quilt. Above them a breeze caught the leaves of the maple, and they sparkled in the late-afternoon sun. From somewhere in the tree, a robin sang and was answered by another on a higher branch.

Mia toddled over to snuggle with her mother, chattering about the birds and grass and Gamma and Gampa's house. Melissa hugged her tiny daughter close. "Just knowing you're here for us," she said to Kate, "even in moments like these"—she turned toward her mother—"that's why I wanted, no, needed, to be here while we're going through all these tests. It's like you and Dad are an anchor, holding us steady through troubled waters."

The sliding door opened, interrupting their conversation, and John and Paul came out to join them. Melissa stayed where she was on the quilt, and John sat down beside her. Kate's arthritic knee was beginning to ache from sitting on the ground, so with a helping hand from Paul, she gratefully got up and took one of the black wrought-iron chairs by the patio table.

Paul disappeared inside the house for a few minutes, then returned with what appeared to be a greeting card and a package the size of a book. A colorful gift bag, stuffed with bright tissue paper, had something that looked like the tips of animal ears peaking over the top.

Paul winked at Kate as he sat down, then smiled at Melissa and John. "Your mother and I wanted to do something special for you two."

He handed the card to Melissa. She opened it with a little squeal, then got up and hugged Paul, then Kate.

"A spa treatment," she sighed. "How could you have known how much I wanted—make that *needed*—this? Thank you so much!"

Paul handed the second package to John, and he pulled out a hardcover book. His eyes lit up when he saw the author's name.

"Grisham's latest," he said. "You couldn't have pleased me more." He stood and shook Paul's hand. "Thank you."

"Last but not least," Paul said and handed the gift bag to Melissa.

Mia sat up and rubbed her eyes. When Melissa pulled a soft stuffed rabbit from the bag, Mia immediately pressed it into her arms, then hurried over to her grandfather and gave him a hug.

She then wrapped her arms around Kate's neck and gave her a kiss on the cheek. "My Gamma," she announced.

"Mia mine," Kate said softly and cuddled her granddaughter close.

Kate met Paul's gaze and tilted her head with wonder . . . and worry. He leaned toward her and whispered, "You were right; it was something we really needed to do."

She started to ask Paul about their finances, then became aware that Melissa and John were watching them. So she just smiled and squeezed his hand. "You are the best dad and grandpa on the planet."

"I second that," Melissa said. She gave Paul another hug.

John leaned back, propping himself with his arms. "So tell us about Mrs. Lambert's urn from Italy. Dad said that you're intrigued by some of its anomalies."

"I made quite a discovery today." Kate went on to tell them about the Etruscan connection and the oddity because the Etruscan culture existed centuries before the time of Saint Francis of Assisi.

They all had questions and comments, then John said, "Where did the Etruscans settle? I mean, where would it be geographically in today's Italy?"

"Tuscany," Kate said. "You can see how the word *Tuscan* evolved from *Etruscan*."

Kate caught Melissa giving Paul a quick raised-eyebrow glance. It was so fleeting, Kate would have missed it if she'd blinked. But then, maybe it was her imagination.

She was still puzzling over it, even as they went on to talk about Kate's son Andrew and his wife Rachel and the latest news about their kids, Ethan and Hannah. Then they touched on Rebecca and her life in New York as a theater understudy.

The tree's shadows were growing longer, and Kate glanced at her watch. "I need to check on the meat loaf," she said, standing.

"Could you bring one of Mia's sweaters out when you come back?" Melissa asked.

Mia was now sitting in her daddy's lap, giggling as he sang the nonsensical *"Mares eat oats and does eat oats and little lambs eat ivy."*

Kate wasn't gone for more than five minutes, but as she looked outside the slider, the three adults' heads were bent toward each other, and they were deep into serious conversation.

The conversation halted abruptly as soon as they heard Kate open the door. Paul flashed the others a warning look, and they immediately fell silent.

Their sheepish expressions told Kate that what she saw this time was *not* her imagination.

THAT NIGHT AS PAUL brushed his teeth, Kate sat down on the edge of the bed and waited for him to come out of the bathroom.

When he did, she said, "You've asked me to trust you. But I must tell you I'm getting pretty worried."

His forehead wrinkled as if he was clueless, but she held up a hand. "I'm serious, Paul. You are keeping something from me, and now you've apparently taken the kids into your confidence."

Paul flushed and came over to sit down beside her. "I'm so sorry you saw us talking," he said. "I thought you'd be in the house much longer."

He was evading her question. Well, she really hadn't asked a question, but she'd certainly implied it.

"So you were busy whispering about something you didn't want me to overhear."

"Well, not exactly . . . I mean, we . . . ah, were just discussing, well, you see . . ."

"I'm your wife, Paul, and I love you. Whatever it is, you need to confide in me. Does it have to do with your health? Did you move the money out of savings because our insurance doesn't cov—"

He stared at her for a moment, unblinking. His expression was filled with compassion, yet he seemed somehow at war with himself, as if wanting desperately to tell her something of utmost importance . . . yet unable to.

In that split second of fear for his health, she tried to picture life without him. A sting of tears crept up the back of her throat.

"Oh, Paul," she said softly, "are you trying to protect me from something?"

He hung his head and didn't answer.

After a moment he looked up. "I asked you before, Katie, and it seems I need to ask you again: please trust me."

"But, Paul—"

He shushed her by putting his index finger over her lips; then standing, he bent to kiss the tip of her nose.

He slid under the covers and turned out the lamp on his bedside table.

Kate sat on the edge of the bed, considering all the possibilities having to do with his health. When people reached later middle age, insurance premiums skyrocketed for a purpose: the incidence of age-related diseases could suddenly come marching into your body without warning.

The missing money, high premiums, and high deductibles all added up to one thing: Paul seemed to be struggling with something that seemed bigger than what they had usually faced.

Finally, she said, "No matter the reason, whatever it is you're keeping from me, I need to know. I love you and want to stand beside you in . . . in whatever it is you're going through."

Without answering he closed his eyes, breathing deeply as if too weary for words.

Kate blinked back her tears and went around to his side of the bed. She touched his forehead with her fingertips, then stooped and kissed his cheek.

"Just let me handle this my own way, Katie," he whispered. "Everything will be okay. I promise. Please, just trust me and don't fret."

Chapter Ten

The next morning, Kate woke before dawn. As she pulled back the covers, she glanced over at Paul's side of the bed, not wanting to wake him. But he wasn't there.

He didn't have any appointments until ten that morning. Why would he be up and out so early? It wasn't like him.

She tiptoed toward the kitchen, wondering why the house was so quiet. Usually, either John or Melissa would have been up by now. Though since they weren't to meet Dr. Lucas at the hospital until one thirty, they certainly had the time to sleep in.

When she reached the kitchen, she was surprised to see that someone had already put on the coffee, and three mugs graced the counter nearby. Three *used* mugs.

Kate reached into the cupboard for another and poured herself a cup of the dark, slightly stale brew.

She peeked into the guest room to see if her suspicions were correct. They were. The port-a-crib was empty. The sleeper sofa was made up, blankets folded.

She went back to the living room, settled into her rocker, and reached for her Bible. She had just opened it to Isaiah, chapter twenty-five, when she heard a light tap at the front door, followed by the sound of the door opening.

"It's just us, Mom," John called to her.

Kate hurried to the entry as he came through the door with their jogger, the three-wheeled stroller that allowed either John or Melissa to jog while pushing it. He was dressed in workout clothes. Mia, in a miniature pastel version of workout sweats, was all smiles and lifted her hands to be picked up. Kate reached for her, and as she pulled her into her arms, the toddler patted Kate's face.

"Gamma!" she pronounced. "Gamma!"

Kate carried her granddaughter into the kitchen. "Are you hungry, Mia mine?"

Mia pointed to Kate's mixer. "Want dat."

"Blue pancakes?" Kate laughed. "I just happen to have some left from yesterday. How about if we warm them up for my special girl?"

She settled Mia into the high chair by the table, then gave her a small plastic bowl of applesauce and a toddler-size spoon while Mia waited for her pancake.

Mia laughed and scooped a spoonful of applesauce into her mouth. It drizzled down her chin.

Kate's heart welled with love for her granddaughter, even as she wiped Mia's face—and her own—with a damp cloth.

The front door opened, and Kate could hear the happy chatter between Paul and Melissa as they came around the corner into the kitchen.

Paul held up a bag of sweet rolls as if it were a trophy. "Look what we brought the family for breakfast. Fresh out of the oven. We've already eaten, but I think we might have our arms twisted to lap a lip over one of these."

Kate gave them each a hug. "So that's where you've been."

"I just wanted to take my daughter to breakfast," he said. "We ended up at the diner just as it opened. These truly are fresh out of the oven."

"We had a great time visiting with LuAnne," Melissa said. "She entertained us with stories of the tour the whole time we were there." She shook her head. "And every other word is in Italian. She said she listened to language tapes for months before they all left and wasn't about to give up using the words she learned just because she's back in the States."

Kate cut the blue pancake into bite-size pieces and put it on a plastic Winnie-the-Pooh plate. After a drizzle of maple syrup, she carried it over to Mia, who was waving her arms like a windmill, applesauce stuck in her hair.

They all stood back in amazement as, with dainty little fingers, she ate one piece after another. Still chomping, she reached for her sippy cup, which John had filled with milk.

"This is the most she's eaten in days," Melissa breathed.

"Maybe it's the syrup," John said. "She doesn't get sweets very often."

Paul winked at Kate. "It's the blue in the pancakes. It always worked with you kids too. Pancakes simply didn't taste the same unless they were blue."

Melissa laughed. "I remember that."

Mia laughed with them and buzzed her lips again, this time with milk.

A FEW HOURS LATER, the kids had bundled Mia in the car and left for their next appointment in Pine Ridge, and Paul soon after backed the pickup out of the driveway for an appointment at church. Kate bustled around the kitchen, cleaning up. Melissa had helped with the breakfast dishes, though because she and Paul had eaten at the diner, there weren't many.

She tried once more to call Dr. Hosea, but an automated voice told her his mailbox was full.

Needing to think things through, she decided to make a batch of brownies, complete with chocolate-fudge frosting.

As she mixed together the ingredients, she thought about the morning. She knew John was in the habit of jogging in the morning, and they had purchased the special stroller so Mia could go with him. She flipped the dial to preheat the oven, then poured the brownie mix into a baking dish. As she waited for the oven to heat, she slid into a chair at the table and considered all the possibilities that came flooding into her mind. One stood out above all the others: Was Paul confiding in Melissa because he was suffering from some disease? With health care costs so high, it would make sense that he would withdraw money from savings. But why would he tell Melissa when she was going through so much herself?

While the brownies baked, she went into her studio, sat down, and sketched a new stained-glass design. She'd had an idea for making a votive candleholder with the images of Francis and Clare, and as she sketched several patterns, Kate considered colors and the shape of the votive. She lost herself in her work, thinking about the lives of these two people and how they had influenced centuries of believers with their radical ideas of following Christ.

One of her favorite quotes was from Francis himself: "Preach Christ, and if you must, use words." It reminded her of another quote, though she couldn't remember if it was attributed to Francis: "You may be the only gospel someone will ever read."

She whispered a prayer, that even in all her concerns for Melissa's family, and her preoccupation with the mystery of the urn, her life would reflect her Lord.

She was almost startled when the oven timer chimed. Almost reluctantly, she left her studio for the kitchen. She had just pulled the brownies from the oven when the phone rang.

It was Livvy, asking for an update on Mia.

Just before the conversation ended, Livvy asked Kate if she could meet for lunch at the park. "I brown-bagged it today," she said. "Enough for two, if you'd like to join me."

"Good timing," Kate said. "I've got a new theory I want to run by you."

She could almost hear her friend smile on the other end of the line. "I love it when that happens," Livvy said.

While the brownies were still warm, Kate used a wooden pick to poke holes across the top. After melting the fudge icing slightly on the stove, she then smoothed it across the warm baked brownies. The kids had always loved the way she made these. The warm icing drizzled into the holes, ensuring moist cookie bars once they were cut.

As she sprinkled on some chopped walnuts, she thought about Dr. Hosea and something that had been niggling at her brain since the middle of the night.

What if the urn was stolen? And if so, from where? A

private collection? A museum? Dr. Hosea had been very excited about the piece. In fact, he'd indicated that the urn didn't look like a copy, that it might be an original. If so, how did it get to the shop where Renee bought it?

She sprinkled another handful of nuts, then paused again.

And if these theories were true, how did Collin Wellington get involved? Did he choose Renee as an unwitting accomplice?

She finished sprinkling the nuts, cut two large pieces for her picnic with Livvy, then covered the rest, still in the baking dish, with cellophane wrap.

KATE WAS WAITING FOR LIVVY at a picnic table, when her friend crossed the street and headed her direction. Four young mothers were having a picnic with their preschoolers a few tables away, and the sounds of their chatter and laughter carried through some young willows. A light breeze rustled the leaves of a nearby maple tree, and a mottled pattern of shade and sunlight danced across the table.

Livvy grinned as she sat down across from Kate. "I hope you like tuna fish." She unwrapped the sandwich and handed half to Kate.

They spoke for a few minutes about the kids, then Livvy leaned forward. "Now, what about your theory?"

Kate told Livvy about what she'd come up with while frosting the brownies.

Livvy blinked. "You think it was stolen? I saw Renee buy it, along with Collin, who inspected it carefully before he gave her the thumbs-up." She untwisted the lid from a bottle of sweetened iced tea, divided it between two paper cups, and handed one to Kate.

She studied Kate thoughtfully, then she leaned forward again and dropped her voice as one of the picnicking mothers walked by with her toddler. "When you're onto something, you're, well, onto something. I take your little nudges seriously. What makes you think it could be stolen?"

"That's actually giving my theory too much credence. Right now, it's just a lilliputian feeling—"

Livvy laughed, and her right eyebrow shot up. "Lilliputian?"

"As in Lilliput, a fictional little guy from the Jonathan Swift nov—"

Livvy was still chuckling. "A librarian would know this."

Kate bit into her sandwich, sobering. After a sip of iced tea, she said, "And this may indeed be fiction, just a gut feeling perhaps, but it makes me want to research recent art thefts or museum heists in Italy . . ."

"Whoa . . ." Livvy sat back, her eyes the size of quarters. "Are we talking about international crime? That's big stuff." She took a bite of sandwich and chewed thoughtfully.

Kate hurried on. "It's a beautiful piece. From the little research I've done online, looking for similar artifacts, it appears to be museum quality. I contacted Dr. Hosea, sent photos, and he got very excited about what he saw.

"In the middle of the night, I woke with a start, first to pray for Mia and wisdom for the doctors who will see her today, then my thoughts flew to the urn. I think Dr. Hosea may know more than what he's told me. Otherwise, why would he get so excited? Why would he take the initiative to contact you so quickly after he saw the article in the *Chronicle*?"

Livvy sipped her tea thoughtfully. "You've got a point."

"He's indicated he wants to see the urn firsthand, run some tests—carbon dating, I suppose."

"That would mean taking it to his university?"

"And telling Renee my suspicions."

"I wonder how she would take that?"

"Well, before I call our Dr. Hosea or tell Renee anything, I want to find out if an urn like this has been reported stolen. I'll start with Florence, since that's where Renee and Collin purchased it, and spread out from there."

A HALF HOUR LATER, Kate was seated at one of the library computers, waiting the few seconds it took for Google to appear.

She tried several combinations of descriptive phrases:

Etruscan urn
Etruscan burial urn
alabaster burial urn Etruscan symbols
alabaster burial urn
Franciscan burial urn alabaster relief

Pages of matches appeared on the search-results screen. She quickly scanned through them, finding dozens of photos of urns, most with relief carvings. Some were from museums, some were from private collections, but none matched Renee's.

She next tried a new angle: "museum heists in Florence."

Nothing.

She did a broader search, including Rome and Milan.

Nothing.

She did another, including all of Italy, then all of Europe.

Nothing.

She sat back, folded her arms, and stared at the screen.

Her middle-of-the-night instincts on this one had obviously been wrong.

Then she pulled up Google once more and typed in: "museum heists in the UK."

Her eyes widened.

A museum in Oxford reported a missing urn nine months earlier . . .

Oxford?

A storm warning slammed into her mind, turning it into a whirlwind of possibilities, dire possibilities, as she considered the implications.

AS SOON AS KATE reached her car, she tried to call Dr. Hosea on her cell phone. This time, when she got his voice mail, she left her number and told him she had new information about the urn and to please call her as soon as possible.

All afternoon and well into the evening, she awaited his call. The phone never played its tune.

By bedtime, she was more puzzled than ever about the urn and its origins, both recent and ancient.

Chapter Eleven

Melissa surprised Kate by fixing breakfast for everyone, insisting that Kate sit down at the kitchen table and relax. Kate watched with wonder as her daughter, who as a teenager stuck up her nose at the very idea of even eating breakfast, fried the bacon, scrambled the eggs, and operated the toaster like a short-order cook.

Kate noticed that Melissa used all egg whites, then added only one yoke to the mix for color before scrambling. When she commented on it, Melissa just smiled. "I just think that Dad—and you, of course, Mom—should keep watching your cholesterol, that's all."

Kate blinked in surprise, then thought about it a moment. "Do you know something you're not telling me?" She glanced at Paul, who had let his gaze drift somewhere over her right shoulder.

Melissa frowned. "What do you mean?"

"About your dad's health."

Melissa smiled gently. "Mom, you both need to take care of yourselves. You're at an age where diet and exercise are all-important. That's all I meant by it. Honest."

Because it was Thursday, the talk over breakfast was about Livvy's latest article in the *Chronicle*, and the picture that accompanied it.

"It's interesting that Livvy featured the urn rather than the folks from Copper Mill," Melissa said, squinting at the photo. She scanned the article, then said, "Ah, but listen to this: 'Tuscany is a place to go with the one you love. Imagine fields of sunflowers stretching as far as the eye can see, their golden petals shimmering in the breeze under an almost purple Tuscan sky.

"'The B and B where we stayed surely must be the most romantic getaway in the world. All of us on the tour agreed that if it hadn't been for missing Assisi, we could have easily spent another week or two in that spot. The food, fixed by the owner's wife, was the best we experienced in all of Italy. And as an added bonus, she spent an afternoon teaching us how to make homemade pasta from start to finish.'"

Most romantic getaway in the world? Kate drew in a deep breath and bit her lower lip as she stood to clear the dishes. "Does she say anything else about the urn, or Renee and Collin?"

"Only that it's on exhibit at the church, and Pastor Paul Hanlon has said everyone is welcome to stop by and see it."

Paul chuckled. "After the press it got in last week's *Chronicle*, I think everyone in Copper Mill has already seen it."

Kate poured coffee all around and slid into her chair.

Mia, sitting in the high chair, lifted her arms and said, "Gamma."

Kate lifted her into her arms. The toddler seemed especially quiet. Popping a binky into her mouth, Mia closed her eyes and snuggled into Kate's lap. For a brief moment, Kate rested her cheek on the toddler's head, her heart once again swelling with love. She wondered how she could think of herself and what she missed in Italy when the needs of Mia, Melissa, and John were so great. She breathed a quick prayer for forgiveness.

"The online version of the article may bring in others," she said, gently combing Mia's hair with her fingers. "Last week's article triggered a response from Dr. Hosea."

"Speaking of which, have you heard from him yet?" Paul took a sip of coffee, watching her over the rim of the mug.

She shook her head. "I'm getting more puzzled by the day."

The phone rang, and eyebrows shot up around the table.

"Maybe that's him," John said.

They all seemed as excited as Kate was over the mystery of the urn's origins. She smiled. It was a good distraction.

Kate reached for the phone. Before she could say hello, Renee asked if she'd seen the morning's *Chronicle*.

"We just finished reading it," Kate told her. "And what a beautiful photograph of the urn. It really shows it off to its best advantage."

"Collin took the shot. He has a camera the size of a credit card, but it takes professional photos."

"He's very good."

Renee chuckled. "His photography is almost as good as his ability to speak all those languages." Without missing a beat, she hurried on. "We're becoming world famous—you know, the urn, Collin, and me. Some friends in Nashville called this morning to congratulate me. They'd seen our picture in front of the Neptune Fountain."

Renee rhapsodized on and on about Collin while John and Paul finished clearing the table and Melissa lifted Mia from Kate's lap to dress her for the trip to Pine Ridge.

After she finished the call with Renee, Kate sat down at the kitchen table to make out a grocery list. Paul came around the corner. He let his gaze drift to the maple tree on the other side of the sliding-glass door, shifted his weight, then cleared his throat.

She tilted her head. "Are you okay?"

He nodded, though a little too quickly. "I'm fine. I just wanted to let you know that I'll be riding in to Pine Ridge with the kids this morning."

Kate stood up with a wide smile. "Oh, good idea! Let's go with them today." She glanced at the clock. "But there's barely time for me to get ready."

"Um . . ." He let his gaze drift again, this time over her left shoulder. "Well, actually, you can't go. That is, I'd *rather* you didn't go."

Kate frowned. "I can't go? You're just going with the kids to the clinic, aren't you?"

Paul's blue eyes met hers. "Actually, no."

She blinked, remembering her promise to trust him.

Melissa came around the corner just then, John right behind her, holding Mia.

Melissa met her father's gaze, then stepped over to Kate and gave her a hug.

"You know, don't you?" Kate said to her daughter.

But Melissa's expression was guileless. "Know what?" she said.

Kate had promised Paul she would trust him, but she hadn't promised not to talk about her worries about him. As soon as John drove away, Melissa beside him in the front seat, Paul looking a little cramped in the back next to Mia's car seat, she hurried to the phone and called Livvy at the library.

"We've got to talk," she said to her friend. "Can you get away for lunch?"

"Is it about the urn?"

"Not this time. It's about Paul, but I can't go into detail right now. I'll tell you when I see you."

"Do you mind going a little early? Say eleven forty-five at the diner? The team from the county's going to be here at one."

"I'll see you there."

KATE ARRIVED AT THE DINER several minutes before Livvy did. She took a seat in their favorite booth.

In the back corner, two men she didn't recognize were having coffee and reading the *Chronicle*. She noticed an ad for the Hamilton Springs Hotel on the bottom left corner of the back page, the same ad she knew was on the page with Livvy's article and the photo of the urn.

The men seemed to be having an exchange about the article, which surprised her.

Livvy breezed through the door just then, distracting Kate. Her friend waved to LuAnne, who sang out, "*Buon giorno*," then headed toward the booth with two menus under one arm, two empty mugs and the coffeepot in her opposite hand. Her pencil rested over one ear, and it looked as if her bright red hair had just been freshened from a bottle. With her polyester dress, spotless apron, and glasses hanging from a jeweled chain around her neck, she looked as if she'd stepped right out of the fifties.

She grinned at the two women. "The chef's special today is spaghetti, though if you want to know the truth, it might as well have come out of a can. You know, that awful stuff kids eat that's shaped like little O's? After you've had the real thing, like we did in Italy, this Americanized stuff will never again make the grade."

"I think I'll pass," Kate said. "How about a dinner salad and half a grilled-cheese sandwich?" She handed the menu back to LuAnne.

"I'll have the same, plus some iced tea."

"Make that two," Kate said.

LuAnne hurried off to put in their orders.

"Okay, spill," Livvy said gently. "You and Paul aren't having trouble, are you?" Her hazel eyes searched Kate's.

"Oh no, it's nothing like that." Kate sat back and folded her arms. "It's just something I can't figure out."

Livvy laughed. "You've just now discovered you can't figure out a man?"

Kate couldn't help smiling. "You've got a point. But this is different. It's about that secret Paul's keeping from me. This morning he took off with the kids and adamantly told me I couldn't go. You know how I am with mysteries . . . This thing is driving me nuts. He's asked me to trust him, and I've given my promise to do so."

In a heartbeat, Livvy's expression changed. The concern was still there, but something else slid in beside it before

Kate could blink. And Livvy was nibbling on her bottom lip, something she did when she was nervous.

"You might try looking at it this way: because you trust him, you don't need to pursue this."

Kate tilted her head and almost asked Livvy to repeat what she'd said. It sounded as if her friend was taking Paul's side in this. "Really?"

Before Livvy could respond, LuAnne returned with their iced teas. She slipped into the booth with them and leaned forward, whispering as she spoke. "Did you see those fellas over there?"

Kate nodded. "I noticed them earlier. They're reading the *Chronicle*. It looked like they were reading about the urn."

"They're actin' pretty shifty, if you ask me," LuAnne said. "They're not from around these parts, I do know that for a fact." She leaned in closer. "They've been talkin' about their boss being on the way to Copper Mill and arguin' about whether to strike while the iron's hot. Those were their very words, strike while the iron's hot."

Kate took another look at the duo. They appeared to be in their thirties. One had carrot red hair; a long, lean face; and a short upper lip. The other sat lower in the booth, signaling to Kate that he was a shorter man by far than the other. He had brown, curly hair and a round face with a goatee and a pencil-thin mustache.

They were still arguing over something when Kate turned back to Livvy and LuAnne.

"They're up to no good," LuAnne whispered. "I've overheard a lot of talkin' in the years I've worked here, I mean *a lot*, and I can call 'em like I see 'em, believe you me. And I'm callin' these two up to no good."

Loretta rang the bell, indicating an order was up, and LuAnne stood to bustle over to get their meals. A minute later, she returned with the sandwiches and salads. Then she searched her pocket for their bill and placed it between the salt and pepper shakers.

"They do look a bit suspicious," Livvy said. Then she laughed. "Though for the life of me, I can't say why."

Kate turned to look, but Carrot-top caught her looking and stared. She gave him a smile and a little wave so she didn't appear to be spying on them.

"They're making some sort of plans on a napkin," she said to Livvy. "Can you see that? It's a drawing, or maybe a map."

"I'm afraid to look," Livvy said. "Every time I do, Curly catches me."

Kate giggled. "Curly? I've been thinking of the other one as Carrot-top."

Livvy giggled with her. "Actually, they don't look very dangerous to me. More like two characters in a Peter Sellers movie." Then she sobered. "Kate, we didn't finish talking about your concerns—with Paul, I mean. I didn't mean to cut you off. You have every right to investigate what he's up to, but I just meant he must have his reasons, and if he's asked you to trust him, well, maybe you ought to consider abiding by his wishes."

Kate nodded. "Today was just so hard. Having them leave without me . . . It really hurt."

Livvy reached across the table to give her a half hug, the only kind of hug that could be managed in a booth. "I know it must have." Then she glanced at the men in the corner and bent forward to whisper, "They're leaving."

Kate grinned. "Shall we follow?"

"I wouldn't miss it for the world."

They pulled out a few bills to cover their lunches and hurried out the door, just behind Curly and Carrot-top, who headed to a late 1960s GTO—metallic blue with a black vinyl top—parked in front of the diner. The paint was faded, and the vinyl top had obviously seen better days.

Carrot-top held out his hand to Curly for the keys.

"You got 'em," Curly said.

"No, no. I gave 'em to you."

They both spoke with backwoods drawls. Carrot-top was at least a foot taller than Curly, who was as round as he was tall.

"Nah," Curly argued. "I'm sure you've got 'em."

They patted their shirt pockets, moved to their pants pockets, then gave each other a blank stare before looking through the front passenger-side window at the steering column.

Kate and Livvy had moved down the sidewalk several feet and stood chatting as if in deep conversation as they watched the duo.

"I think they've locked themselves out of the car," Kate said, stifling a giggle.

"Maybe we should offer to call a locksmith," Livvy said.

Just then, the men's voices rose, and Carrot-top moved menacingly closer to Curly. "You're always messin' up," he said. "Remember that other time? You went off and left the car unlocked and the keys in the ignition."

"That was the boss's fault," Curly said. "He had me so

nervous, I wasn't thinkin' straight that day. It was his fault the car got stolen."

"Yeah? He didn't think so. He's given us one last chance to make up for it, and now look what you did."

They stared at the ignition for another few seconds, then rounded the car, one around the front, the other around the back, only to literally bump into each other by the driver's side door.

Both shook their heads and rolled their eyes as if blaming the other for being a dolt. Then Curly pulled out one of those little kits that thieves use to open just about any lock they might meet, and within three seconds, the duo was in the car. The engine rumbled, and the tailpipe popped like gunfire as they drove off.

Kate and Livvy looked at each other.

"What was that all about?" Livvy said, shaking her head.

"LuAnne may be right. These two might be up to no good."

"But what?" Livvy said. Then her eyes widened. "They were looking at the article in the *Chronicle*."

"Specifically the photograph." Kate swallowed hard. "And of course, the article mentions where the urn is on display."

"What should we do?"

"I don't know that there's anything we can do. We don't have any evidence—real evidence, I mean—that they have anything to do with them."

"It's just a souvenir," Livvy said.

"Or is it?" Kate narrowed her eyes in thought. "Even if it is just a souvenir, it's special to Renee, and for that reason alone, we can't let anything happen to it. I'll call Skip and let him know what we observed."

Livvy checked her watch, started to turn toward the library, then stopped and touched Kate's hand. "We got so busy with everything else, I forgot to ask about Mia. What's the latest?"

"I haven't heard anything since this morning."

Almost as if on cue, her cell phone chimed. She checked caller ID, then held up a hand for Livvy to wait and mouthed, "It's Paul," as she flipped it open.

"I'm with the kids, Katie. We're about to start for home."

"That's good. I'll start thinking about dinner."

"There's something else."

"What is it?"

For several heartbeats, he didn't speak. When he finally did, his voice was full of sorrow. "The preliminary results of the tests have come in."

Chapter Twelve

Kate was getting ready for church when the phone rang. She heard Paul pick it up in the kitchen, but after his initial "hello," he did more listening than talking. She ran the brush through her hair, dabbed on some lip gloss, then hurried to the kitchen to see who had called. She rounded the corner just as Paul hung up the phone.

"That was Sheriff Roberts," he said, turning toward Kate. "He said that after you called Skip Spencer about these guys at the diner, the deputy's been keeping an eye on the church, just in case. Sure enough, last night around midnight he spotted a man standing by the church entrance. But by the time Skip got out of his SUV, he'd run off. Skip sounded worried, said to thank you for the heads-up. He plans to keep an eye on the church for the next few nights."

AN HOUR LATER, Kate settled into the second pew, Mia on her lap, Melissa on her left, and John on Melissa's opposite side. After a rousing "Holy, Holy, Holy, Lord God Almighty," with Sam Gorman at the organ, Paul stepped to the pulpit and asked Melissa and her family to stand. John took Mia into his arms, then stood and faced the congregation, Melissa at his side.

"We would like to ask for you all to pray with us through this week," Paul said solemnly. "We've just found out that Mia may have to undergo open-heart surgery to repair a valve that isn't opening and closing correctly. This means that the blood can't flow smoothly, and she isn't getting the oxygen she needs in her lungs."

Gasps rose from the congregation. Kate heard more than one "Oh no," and someone sitting in the pew behind her patted her on the shoulder.

Then Mia, without knowing what she was doing, changed the tone of the service and the expressions on faces from concern and sorrow to smiles and even a few giggles. While her grandpa was explaining her condition to the congregation, she made a face at her daddy, patted his cheek, then played with his ears.

Renee Lambert was sitting behind Kate, Kisses on her lap, and Mia giggled and tried to squirm out of her daddy's arms to reach the little Chihuahua.

"Doggie," she squealed. "Doggie!"

Renee, in a surprising move, reached beneath the pew and handed the end of Kisses' leash to Kate. A minute later, the little dog trotted beneath the pew and hopped on Kate's lap.

Mia reached noisily for her "gamma," and soon Kate was holding her granddaughter too, who was happily hugging Kisses. The Chihuahua's tail thumped with delight as Mia played with his ears.

John and Melissa sat down, and the service proceeded. Two more hymns were sung, one by the choir. Kate didn't take her usual place with them because she didn't want to disturb Mia, who had popped in her favorite binky and was falling asleep, her head nestled in the crook of Kate's arm. Kisses had curled up beside her, and Kate prayed he wouldn't raise the rafters with his usual snoring.

"I would like for us to consider God's strength this morning," Paul said when he stood to give the sermon. "The kind of strength we need when our world is rocked off its axis by unexpected and unwelcome events."

He paused, looking out across the congregation. "In Psalm 46:1–2, we read, 'God is our refuge and strength, a very present help in trouble.' Friends, sooner or later, we all get hit with events that bring us to our knees. Those unexpected events that trouble us or those we love."

He named some of the challenges that members of the congregation were facing, then his gaze rested on his family, especially on Mia, who was now sound asleep in Kate's arms.

Paul's sermon was one of the most heartfelt Kate had ever heard him give, and she knew he was talking to himself as much as he was to the congregation. Each time he spoke of needing God's grace, strength, and courage to continue on, he glanced at Mia, and something in his face told Kate what a struggle he was having over the news about her surgery.

"When our days seem dark," he concluded, "we can take comfort that God knows our every thought . . . that he feels our every pain . . . that he cares about us every bit as much as he cares about the birds of the air."

He paused. "And if there is anything we can learn from the Scriptures, it is that God's faithfulness is something we can count on more than anything else in life.

"So, this morning, I say to you with the psalmist, 'Be of good courage, and He shall strengthen your heart, all you who hope in the Lord.'"

He looked out across the congregation again, then moved to stand once more behind the pulpit. "Without a doubt, the greatest comfort of all," Paul said, "and that which can give us the most enduring strength in the midst of trouble, is the fact that we are never alone—we or those we love—no matter the circumstances we are going through. God, in his everlasting faithfulness, is with us."

THAT AFTERNOON, Kate again spread the quilt beneath the maple tree. The family had just finished eating a chicken-and-tortilla casserole that Kate had put in the oven before church, and as she sat down with Mia, Melissa came out to sit with her. She brought two glasses of iced tea and handed one to Kate.

The men were sitting at the kitchen table, John's laptop open in front of them. The sliding door leading outside was pushed back, with only the screen pulled closed. Kate could hear John's rapid typing as he opened a new program that he wanted to show his father-in-law.

"How are you doing?" she asked Melissa.

"Dad's sermon really spoke to my heart. I felt he'd written it just for John and me." She fell quiet a moment, then said, "But honestly, I don't feel very courageous at all right now. What if Mia does have to have surgery? She's so tiny."

A balmy late-spring breeze rustled the leaves overhead, and a couple of sparrows hopped along the grass in the corner of the yard. A moment later, a mockingbird sang from a nearby tree, then fluttered over to land in the maple tree above them, its tail bobbing jauntily.

"This morning, one little portion of a verse stood out above all the others your dad quoted."

Melissa absently stroked Mia's forehead as the child rested in Kate's lap. She gave Kate a questioning look.

"'Be of good courage, and he shall strengthen your heart.'" She smiled at Melissa. "When I heard the words, I substituted Mia's name: 'Be of good courage, and he shall strengthen Mia's heart.'"

Melissa's eyes grew wide in wonder. "Yes," she said quietly, her eyes filling. "My prayer will be that he will strengthen my baby's heart. Just whispering those words gives me courage."

Just then, the telephone rang, and Paul reached for it. Again, it seemed that Paul was doing more listening than talking.

Kate gave Melissa a quizzical look. "I wonder who that could be?"

Her daughter shrugged and let her gaze drift away from Kate's. Melissa obviously knew more than she was willing to let on.

Paul hung up the phone then got up and came over by the sliding screen door. "I need to run an errand," he said.

Kate couldn't imagine what could be so important that it couldn't wait until Monday. She sometimes even resented such intrusions into their Sunday afternoons. After all the energy Paul put out on Sunday mornings, he needed to rest in the afternoon.

Noting Kate's frustration, Paul said, "I'm sorry. It's just something I need to do."

"I was about to suggest that we babysit and let the kids have some time to themselves."

"Actually, I don't think it will take both of you to watch Mia," Melissa said. "She's worn out from her busy Sunday morning." She lifted the sleeping toddler into her arms, stood, and reached for Kate's hand to help her up. "But I think we'll take you up on your offer. A banana split from Emma's Ice Cream Shop has been calling my name since we got here."

Kate shook out the quilt as Melissa stepped into the house, Mia curled on her shoulder. John went with her to settle Mia in the port-a-crib, which they'd moved into the living room, saying something about walking instead of driving to the ice cream shop.

Paul stepped outside to help Kate fold the quilt. They worked as a team, folding the quilt in neat squares until they stood a foot apart.

His eyes met hers, and he gave her a sheepish grin.

She shook her head slowly, sighed, and smiled back. She couldn't help it.

KATE STIRRED UP a batch of her oatmeal orange-cranberry cookies, her thoughts returning to the urn and how it came to be in Renee's hands. Something had been niggling at the back of her brain about how Renee and Collin met—and how fast the romance was moving. It hadn't even been three weeks since they met.

She slipped the first cookie sheet into the oven, set the timer, and turned on the burner under the teakettle. Then she took a few minutes to check on Mia, who was still sleeping soundly, and headed back to the kitchen.

As she pulled a teacup and saucer out of the cupboard, her thoughts again went back to Renee. She had heard bits and pieces of Renee's history, but she realized she didn't know many of the details about her background, her marriage, or the untimely death of her husband. Though more times than not, Renee rubbed her the wrong way, Kate's heart went out to her. Collin must have been even more charming than Kate could imagine for Renee to have fallen so suddenly for him.

The teakettle whistled, and she stood to pour the boiling water over the Earl Grey loose-leaf tea that Renee had given her. She had only poured in a drizzle when she stopped, another thought flying into her brain. Could Renee have met Collin before?

Was their meeting truly serendipitous? Or had "bumping into her" been planned?

Something clicked, and she stopped dead still. She was missing something, but what was it? One thing she needed to consider: Renee, unwittingly, likely held some clues.

She put the teakettle back on the stove, glanced in at Mia, then she headed to the phone.

She would invite Renee over for tea and a chat. It was time to delve a little deeper into Renee's early life.

Chapter Thirteen

Renee wasted no time driving over to Kate's. Kate led her into the kitchen, and they sat down at the table, where Kate had already set out her best teapot and teacups with some pretty floral napkins she'd bought at the Mercantile. A plate of fresh-baked cookies was in the center of the table, the scent of cinnamon, nutmeg, and ginger still filling the kitchen.

"My, my," Renee said. "What is the occasion?" Kisses jumped into her lap, circled a couple of times, then settled down.

"I'm babysitting Mia. My family's off running hither and yon, and I decided I was in the mood for cookies and tea and someone to share them with."

Without commenting, Renee lifted the lid and peered into the contents of the teapot. Kate grinned and passed the plate of cookies.

Renee took a cookie and munched thoughtfully.

"Did I tell you that my Collin can fix the perfect cup of tea? Even while we were in Italy, he found loose-leaf Earl Grey and Devonshire cream, if you can imagine."

Kate sipped her tea, then reached for a cookie. "Maybe he can give us all some instructions on how to make the perfect cup of English tea. Has he said when he's coming?"

"He hasn't booked his flight, but he's hoping to get away before the end of the month."

"I ran into your mother again the other day. Seems she's still having a hard time with all this."

Renee put down her teacup. "She's afraid of losing me." She shrugged and looked away from Kate toward the maple tree in the backyard. "And she knows how hard it was when I lost Ellis, even though it was years ago."

"Ellis was your husband?"

"Yes. We went to college together. He had a dream to become a doctor, which suited me just fine. I knew I'd make the perfect doctor's wife."

She picked up her teacup, pinkie finger extended, and raised an eyebrow. "I anticipated the social events I would be expected to attend and host. I knew without a doubt I would be a hit, which would have benefited us both."

Kate poured more tea, but Renee seemed lost in thought and didn't notice. "It's been a long time since I've thought about all this, but every time I do, I realize that Ellis has never left my heart.

"Anyway, I dropped out of college and went to work to bring in a paycheck while Ellis continued in medical school. The same year he got his MD, I got pregnant. We had a beautiful little girl we named Caroline—for obvious reasons—though we called her Carrie."

She stopped speaking for a moment, patting Kisses, who

was snoring lightly in her lap. "There was this accident . . . a freak thing, really. Our little girl ran into the street . . . a car was coming . . ."

Renee's eyes filled, and again she looked away from Kate.

Kate reached for her hand. "If this is too painful, please don't feel you need to—"

Renee blew her nose and turned back to Kate. "My mother's concern for me, I think, is based on the fear that I might lose someone I love again." She shrugged and dabbed at her eyes. "And maybe fear that she'll lose someone she loves too." She gave Kate a watery smile.

"To make a long story short, to try to fill the void, I returned to school to get my degree. Ellis, now a surgeon, lost himself in his work and also, to ease some of his own pain, began going with a group of doctors to donate his services as a surgeon to the poor in other countries. Then one day on a trip to some remote village in Guatemala, his plane went down. It was monsoon season, and the pilot didn't use good judgment. The wreckage was never found.

"He'd wanted me to go with him on the trip, but I needed to study for a final."

She shifted her gaze to the little Chihuahua in her lap for a moment before looking up again. She nibbled her cookie and took a sip of tea. "It took me years to forgive Ellis for going on that trip—and to forgive God for all I'd lost. First Carrie, who'd been the light of both of our lives, then Ellis, who was my soul mate."

"I'm so sorry," Kate said.

Renee sniffed, and the haughty expression she so often

wore returned in a heartbeat. "Well, there was a silver lining in all this. Ellis had taken out a large life insurance policy that left me quite nicely fixed for the rest of my life. And without going into detail, I must say I've made some wise investments over the years . . . not to mention my philanthropic work with various charities. Though I try to keep that particular candle under a bushel here in Copper Mill."

"I understand why it would be so hard to give your heart to another man," Kate said. "Collin must be very special."

She nodded. "He is. Though, as with all men, he'll need a little training," she added.

"What's surprising is that it all happened so fast. I mean, you knew Ellis for years before you married . . ."

"Well, you see, even Collin has said it's as if we'd known each other forever. And that urn. When he chose it, it was exactly as if he knew my likes and dislikes. As if we'd known each other before."

"Could it be possible that you had met bef—"

A cry from the port-a-crib interrupted her. Kate stood up like a shot and went over to the crib.

Mia lay still, looking up at Kate with feverish eyes. Her cheeks were flushed, and her breathing seemed too rapid.

"Oh, dear Lord," Kate whispered and reached for the toddler.

In a split second, Renee was at her side. She retrieved the blankie from the port-a-crib and tucked it around Mia while Kate shifted the toddler to her opposite shoulder.

"Does Paul have his cell phone on him?" Renee asked, her face white.

Kate nodded.

Without hesitation, Renee ran to the kitchen and dialed the number as Kate called it out to her. "Come quickly," Renee said, her tone clipped. "It's Mia!"

As Renee rounded the corner, Kate sat down and settled Mia's head against the crook of her arm. Renee knelt beside her. As the older woman gazed down at the toddler's face, she reached out and brushed a blonde lock of hair from her forehead with her fingertips. Then her eyes met Kate's, and in that instant, Kate knew she was thinking of Carrie, the precious child she had lost.

Just then, Paul, John, and Melissa came in the front door.

Melissa ran over and knelt on the other side of the rocker. John was a half step behind her. "Call Dr. Lucas' emergency number," she said as she reached for Mia. "Hurry."

But John had punched in the numbers before the words were spoken.

Chapter Fourteen

How long has it been?"

Paul looked up from the *Newsweek* he was flipping through, then checked his watch. "About forty-five minutes."

"It seems like hours." Kate sighed. "Waiting is always so difficult."

Just then, Melissa came into the waiting room and headed toward them. She sat down next to Paul. "Thank you both for coming. It meant a lot to us to know you were right there behind us on our way."

She took a deep breath. "Mia is stable, actually sitting up and smiling. Dr. Lucas fitted her with an oxygen mask to ease her breathing and make her more comfortable. He wants to keep her here for observation."

"I agree that it's the best thing," Kate said. "Is he calling in some other specialists?"

Melissa smiled. "How did you know that before we did?"

"Simple deduction. If the tests he's run are inconclusive, it makes sense he would call in someone else."

"Dr. Lucas wants to avoid surgery if at all possible, and rather than putting Mia through the trauma of moving to another hospital or clinic for more tests, he's called another pediatric cardiologist who will be here tomorrow. He's part of the team we mentioned earlier."

Paul sat forward. "It's the waiting, the not knowing what's ahead, that's the hardest." He gave his daughter a gentle smile. "It's difficult for your mother and me, but I can only imagine what it's like for you and John."

Melissa tucked an errant strand of hair behind one ear. Her eyes looked heavy with concern. "We're going to stay with her, of course," she said. "They've got recliners in the pediatric room for parents."

"Can we see her before we leave?" Paul asked.

Melissa stood. "She's wide awake and will love seeing you."

A few minutes later, they peered through the doorway of the brightly colored room. Mia was sitting in a crib jabbering to the stuffed rabbit that Paul had picked out for her.

She looked up and giggled as Kate and Paul walked toward her, then she held up her arms to be picked up. Being careful with the oxygen-mask tubes and connections, Paul lifted her from the crib, held her close, then as the rest of the family circled around him, he prayed for the child in his arms.

IT WAS NEARLY MIDNIGHT when Paul and Kate headed home.

Paul reached across the space between them to take Kate's hand. "You okay?"

"I'm just thinking about the kids and all they're going through, and of course, mostly about our little Mia."

"Being a parent is hard, but being a grandparent is in some ways harder."

They rode along in silence for a few minutes. Then Paul said, "Tell me the latest about the urn. We've been so concerned about Mia, I haven't had a chance to ask."

Kate pulled her knees up onto the seat and turned toward him. "I'm still waiting to hear from Dr. Hosea. Meanwhile, my curiosity about the piece is growing stronger by the day. I invited Renee over this afternoon, thinking I might find out more about the urn and the man who talked her into buying it. But we ended up talking more about her life story than anything else." Kate paused in thought. "Still, something about the way she met Collin Wellington bothers me, but I can't explain what."

"Did she tell you anything new?"

"Only that they both agreed it felt as if they'd known each other for years. Renee said she was amazed at how well he seemed to know her likes and dislikes, and how similar to his they were."

She narrowed her eyes in thought as Paul slowed the car and turned onto the highway leading to Copper Mill. "It seems almost too perfect."

Paul's eyebrow shot up. "What do you mean?"

"Honestly, I don't know. There's just something about this whirlwind romance that makes me curious. And after hearing about Renee's background, my heart goes out to her. No wonder her mother is so concerned. I don't want to see her get hurt."

Paul gave her a quizzical look, and she told him what Renee had divulged that afternoon. She could see by his expression that he had a new appreciation for her.

She leaned forward. "But something else came up in my latest sleuthing on the Net. When I did a search for museum thefts, one came up in Oxford."

Paul glanced at her, his eyebrow raised. "Oxford?"

"Exactly. The description of the urn was identical to Renee's. And then there's my uneasiness about Collin."

"You're not thinking he stole the urn, are you?"

Kate sighed. "I can't imagine that he did. But just as the old saying goes, 'All roads lead to Rome,' it seems all my curious musings lead to Collin."

"And now you're worried that he might be preying on Renee's affections, that he's using her."

"I don't want to believe that, but I am worried."

Paul turned onto Smoky Mountain Road, and as the Honda rounded the curve and the parsonage came into sight, Kate leaned her head back wearily.

They got out of the car, and as they were walking into the house, Paul reached out for Kate's hand and stopped her. "I've been wanting to tell you something for a while now," he said.

She tilted her head.

"You've shown so much grace with how you handled things after I insisted we back out of the trip to Italy. I know how much you wanted to go. I just want you to know how much I appreciated it. It's made some other . . . issues . . . easier to deal with."

"I'd rather be with you here, Paul Hanlon, than anywhere else on earth," she said softly. "Other women might need to be walking through a field of sunflowers under a Tuscan sky, or splashing barefoot in Trevi Fountain, or following the footsteps of Saint Francis in Assisi." She looked up at him and touched his cheek. "But just hug me tight, my dearest, and I'm in heaven."

And Paul did just that.

AS KATE STEPPED through the door into the kitchen, she noticed that there was a message on their answering machine. She went over to it and scowled as she listened to a barely discernable whispered message.

"I need to see you, and I'll not take no for an answer . . ."

"Who is it?" Paul was already in his pajamas standing in the doorway.

"I have no idea," Kate said. "I'll listen again."

Paul came over to stand beside her as she replayed the message.

"It's of vital importance," the gravelly whisper went on. "You might say it's a life-and-death issue."

Chapter Fifteen

By morning, Kate had realized that the mysterious voice on their answering machine belonged to Caroline Beauregard Johnston.

She waited until ten o'clock to call.

Renee answered and seemed surprised when Kate asked to speak to her mother.

"Who is this?" Caroline demanded a moment later.

"Kate Hanlon."

"I've been waiting for your call," Caroline wheezed.

Kate strained to hear the older woman's voice. "Do you have a cold?"

"Goodness, no. I just don't want to be overheard, if you know what I mean. I need to talk with you—away from the house—for obvious reasons."

What obvious reasons? Then it dawned on her. Caroline didn't want Renee to overhear the conversation. That meant it probably had to do with Collin Wellington.

"You can pick me up in twenty minutes," the voice continued. "I'll be waiting at the corner of Sweetwater and Ashland.

Synchronize your watch with mine. It's exactly 10:13. I'm leaving right now." She hung up without saying good-bye.

Kate sat back with a sigh. Two things nagged at her. First, she had planned to intensify her efforts to get in touch with Dr. Hosea that morning. Second, she didn't like going behind Renee's back, no matter the reason. But she couldn't leave Caroline standing alone on the street corner.

First things first. She would pick up Caroline, listen to her concerns, then try to smooth things over between mother and daughter. From past experience, Kate knew that the task was likely mission impossible. She sent up a quick prayer.

She didn't have much more time than what it took to pull on a favorite jean skirt and cotton sweater, run a brush through her hair, and race out the door.

She glanced at her watch as she backed the Honda out of the garage, feeling a little silly that she actually had synchronized it with Caroline's.

SHE PULLED UP to the curb beside Caroline. As usual, Caroline was wearing her straw hat with its froth of silk flowers. With her frilly summer dress and white cardigan sweater, she was the perfect portrait of a genteel Southern woman.

"We'll go to Emma's Ice Cream," she announced as Kate helped her into the car. "I don't expect my daughter will drop in there. Not that she doesn't like a fudge sundae once in a while, but she's writing a letter to . . . that man."

"All right," Kate sighed. "Emma's it is." She pulled away from the curb.

"Don't go back down Ashland," she said, peering out the passenger-side window. "We might be seen."

Kate turned onto Sweetwater.

"You're driving too fast," Caroline said, silk flowers bobbing. "It's making me nervous."

Kate slowed the car and crept along until she reached Main Street. A few seconds later, she parked in front of the ice-cream shop. She got out of the car, rounded the back, and then opened the door for Caroline, who exited the vehicle like a queen. She unfolded her jeweled cane, tucked one hand around the crook of Kate's elbow, and tapped along the sidewalk, the cane in the other hand.

They had almost reached the entrance to Emma's when Kate spotted a metallic blue GTO parked in front of the Mercantile.

She stopped to gape. The car was empty, which meant the duo she'd seen the other day was either in one of the other shops . . . or in the ice-cream shop.

"What?" Caroline demanded, following her gaze.

"Nothing really. I just recognized a car from the other day."

"That GTO?"

"Yes."

"Looks like the ones that ran moonshine back in the day. It's a sixty-eight, I would guess."

Kate grinned. Caroline might have been ninety-something, but she knew her cars.

Kate held open the door, and Caroline sailed through, placed her order at the counter, demanding it be brought to their table, then made her way across the small room.

Emma Blount, the owner, stood behind the counter, shaking her head. "That's a woman who knows where she's goin'," she whispered to Kate.

Kate nodded with a grin, placed her own order, then followed Caroline to a small round table.

Kate started to sit down, then noticed Carrot-top and Curly sitting at a corner table. There were enough other customers in the shop to make Kate's arrival at the table less obvious. But she needn't have worried. The duo was lost in conversation and didn't so much as glance in her direction.

Caroline leaned forward. "Those two belong to the moonshine car is my guess," she whispered. "And since you were agape at their wheels, I thought you'd want to be within earshot." She surprised Kate with a wink.

Kate swallowed her smile.

"Is this a stakeout?" Caroline whispered, sounding exactly like her daughter.

Kate laughed. "Not at all. Let's just call them persons of interest."

Caroline's eyes brightened. "I've got real good hearing when I want to. I'll let you know what I pick up."

Did this mean she heard what she wanted to and played deaf to the rest? Kate wondered if Renee knew this about her mother.

This was turning into a much more entertaining ice-cream adventure than she had anticipated.

"They're talking about what flavors they want," Caroline reported. "One wants a double scoop of pistachio, cone on the side." She cocked her head and narrowed her eyes in concentration. "The other one is on a diet. Wants frozen yogurt. No cone. Now they're arguing about which one has to go to the counter to place their order and pick up the goods."

"The goods?"

"You know, the ice cream and yogurt."

"I think I know which is which," Kate said. Then she leaned in closer. "You must have something important to tell me after going to all this trouble to get me here without your daughter knowing."

Caroline sighed deeply. "It's that man Renee is planning to marry."

"You really think she's going to marry him?"

"Of course. Anybody can see that she's gaga over him, carrying on the way she is. And at her age." She shook her head slowly. "If he really cared about Renee, he would have seen to it that she picked something of value. Like crystal or jewelry. Instead, he insisted she buy that urn—a crematory urn, or whatever it's called." She visibly shuddered. "What kind of a romantic gesture is that? Besides, this whole urn business, showing it off at your church like it's some valuable antique, just proves that someone's trying to pull the wool over my daughter's eyes."

She leaned in closer and dropped her voice. "Since you're Renee's best friend, I thought she might listen to you. It's not just the urn I'm concerned about; it's that man."

Renee's best friend? Kate swallowed hard, then thought about it. Renee too often rubbed people the wrong way and didn't have many close friends. Caroline may be right.

Caroline continued. "I thought of another reason he wants to marry her. I saw it on TV." She sat back and folded her arms across her chest. Her eyes snapped when she said, "Citizenship."

Kate blinked. "Citizenship?"

"That's right."

They both fell quiet as Emma brought their ice creams.

"Like I said, I've seen it on TV. Men marry women to gain US citizenship. That man probably wants to marry Renee so he can live in the country legally."

Kate took a spoonful of ice cream, vanilla with fresh strawberries, remembering the sorrow in Renee's history and considering Caroline's possibly unfair assessment.

"But isn't it equally possible that someone could fall in love with Renee just because of who she is?" she asked gently.

Caroline gave her a sharp look, then something in the back of her eyes softened. "Yes, of course. It happened with her dear Ellis." She daintily cut the bananas in her banana split into bite-size pieces. "My daughter does have her lovable moments."

"And perhaps after you meet Collin, you'll feel differently," Kate said. "Getting to know him during his visit may give you a whole different perspective—of him personally and how he treats Renee."

"*Hmmph*," Caroline said. "Time will tell."

As Kate took a few more bites of ice cream, it occurred to her that she should ask herself the same question about Renee. Could someone love her just because of who she was? What if the whole incident with the urn was nothing more than what it seemed—two people meeting and falling in love?

Yes, to some, she concluded, Renee could be lovable, but in this case, Kate still had the suspicion that love was just another element in the mystery. There was something more to it; she could feel it in her bones.

"They're saying they just ought to get it done," Caroline said, her eyes squinted closed in concentration.

It took Kate a moment to figure out what she meant.

Then Caroline went on. "'We gotta wait for the boss,'" one of them just said." She scooped up a piece of banana, dipped it in chocolate sauce, then popped it into her mouth. "'Easy as taking candy from a baby.' That's from the other one."

Though Kate was facing the men, Caroline was close enough to hear more clearly what they were saying. Kate feigned disinterest as Caroline reported their conversation. With each new phrase, the dots began to connect: the same duo in the diner, poring over the article about the urn four days ago; the man Skip saw running from the front steps of the church; the urn that might be of priceless value, according to Dr. Hosea.

"'I wonder what's takin' the boss so long to get here. Somethin' must've come up,'" Caroline reported in a barely discernable whisper, her eyes sparkling as she continued, "'We're pretty smart,'" one of them is saying, "'Maybe he doesn't expect us to wait. I say let's go for it.'"

Kate couldn't help herself; she gave a quick look to the speaker. At the same instant, Carrot-top and Curly caught her stare, blinked as if suddenly recognizing her—and without a word slapped some bills on the table and bolted for the door, leaving half-eaten ice cream and frozen yogurt on the table.

"Goodness," Caroline said. "Was it something we said?"

"Wait here," Kate said, then scooting out of her chair, she moved quickly to the front window.

She watched as they bumbled across the street to the

GTO, only to halt and round the car, trying the doors. Words were exchanged with great animation, then Carrot-top gave Curly a shove and pointed at the ice-cream-shop door.

"You left the keys on the table, you dolt," he said, loud enough for the entire shop to hear.

Curly's shoulders slumped as he patted down his pockets again. Kate watched as he shuffled back across the street, came inside, only to return to the car a few minutes later jangling the keys and grinning.

In a matter of seconds, off they roared, a rumbling flash of metallic blue and black vinyl.

Kate went back to join Caroline, whose banana-split dish looked as if it had been licked clean. The older woman smiled up at her. "You can take me home. I feel much better now that we've had this heart-to-heart and I know you will handle it with Renee."

Kate helped her stand and steadied her as she unfolded her cane. "I am upset with you about one thing, though," Caroline added as they made their way to the door.

"What's that?"

"I wish I'd seen those persons of interest take off in that GTO. I could hear the engine rumble from in here, but that's just not the same as watching it in person."

AFTER DROPPING CAROLINE off at her home, Kate headed to the library. She pulled the Honda into the parking lot, then trotted through the entrance and up the stairs to the computer bank.

Caroline had her own reasons for mistrusting Collin, and

without realizing it, had also made Kate's concerns march back into her brain, front and center. She Googled "Oxford University," then sat back as the Web site loaded. She quickly scanned the menu, making her way through their various departments: administration, communications, security, governance, welfare, and myriad others.

Finally, she spotted human resources. She clicked on the information screen and sent an e-mail asking how she might obtain copies of papers Collin had authored on ancient burial urns, particularly those from the Etruscan era through the twelfth century. She typed her name and contact information at the bottom of the e-mail.

Next, she e-mailed Dr. Hosea, this time requesting a return receipt indicating the time and date the e-mail was opened on his end.

Before she logged off, she received an answer from Oxford:

> Dear Mrs. Hanlon,
>
> It is our policy to forward questions such as yours directly to the employee, or retired employee, as in this case. We have forwarded your e-mail to Professor Wellington.

Kate's eyes widened. That was something she hadn't expected. What if Collin told Renee someone from Copper Mill had made inquiries about his work? Someone named Kate Hanlon. She shivered, wondering why the prospect bothered her so. After all, she only inquired about papers he'd written. Somehow, even that self-explanation didn't give her comfort.

She clicked on the home-page Web site, again planning to log off the computer. Then she noticed the Breaking World News column and stopped, her hand hovering over the mouse.

> *Second heist thwarted in Oxford museum.* Suspects are still at large and thought to be part of an international ring concentrating on priceless antiquities. This is the second such break-in at the Exeter Museum of Art and Antiquities, and the seventh worldwide. A spokesperson for Scotland Yard says the agency has doubled its efforts to apprehend the thieves and is teaming with the FBI and other law-enforcement agencies in the United States and Western Europe.

Kate moved closer to the monitor and reread the article. No further details were given, but as she sat back, her mind was spinning as if she'd clicked on some sort of brain rewind and fast-forward buttons at the same time.

And at the center of the vortex was the one person who seemed to have started it all.

Chapter Sixteen

Kate glanced at the library clock, then pulled out her cell phone and dialed Renee. "I need to talk with you," she said when Renee answered.

There was a short pause followed by an indignant sniff. "I've been waiting for you to call and explain."

Kate frowned. "Explain?"

"About secretly meeting with my mother this morning."

That wasn't why Kate had called, but it was something she did need to talk to Renee about. "Would you like to meet at my house for lunch?"

"Actually, it's my turn to have you over. Why don't you stop by, and I'll put a little something together for an early lunch. I just dropped Mama off to visit her friends at Green Acres, so we can speak privately."

Kate agreed and disconnected the call. It was barely eleven o'clock, and she felt she'd lived through a week since she backed out of the driveway this morning.

RENEE HAD SET UP A TABLE in her backyard flower garden. A pale pink linen tablecloth covered it, with a darker pink set of place mats and linen napkins. In the center was a small vase of pink and white roses. A small platter of finger sandwiches had been placed to one side of the arrangement; a colorful medley of melon balls graced the other side in a sparkling glass bowl.

"Why, this is beautiful, Renee," Kate said. "Absolutely beautiful."

Renee blushed, something as rare as her smile. "Actually, the table and chairs are a new purchase. Catalog order. And the menu is a trial run for when Collin gets here. I was already working on these when you called."

She went over to the table and picked up one of the rectangular sandwiches with sterling-silver tongs. "Cream cheese and watercress. See what you think." She handed it to Kate.

Kate took a bite. "Delicious."

Renee gestured for her to sit down. "And here's an egg salad with a touch of curry and fresh dill."

Using the tongs, Kate placed one on her plate. Between them, Kisses sat on his hind legs to beg. Renee popped half a cream-cheese-and-watercress sandwich into his mouth.

"The herbs are good for his digestive system," she said to Kate. Without missing a beat, she went on. "Now this is truly an amazing one—pumpernickel with smoked salmon and a touch of cream cheese. Try it."

They ate in silence for a few minutes, then Renee narrowed her eyes. "What's going on with Mama?"

Kate shot up an arrow prayer for wisdom and grace. "She's very worried about you . . . worried that things have happened too fast with Collin."

Renee raised an eyebrow. "As if I'm not a big enough girl to make wise decisions."

Kate chuckled to break the tension. "As a mom, I think I'll worry about my children even after I'm ninety. Your mother's no different."

Renee dished the melon balls into a small glass bowl shaped like an apple and handed it to Kate. "She's made no secret of the fact that she can't stand him, yet she's never even met him. She's been all over town telling people that he's out to get my money or plans to use me to get US citizenship. You name it, she's thought of it."

So Renee *did* know about the accusations; that made Kate feel even worse. "People who know you won't believe a word of it, believe me. They know you to be a savvy, thinking, deliberate woman. And I think they also realize that your mother is afraid of losing you after all these years."

Renee shot her an appreciative look. "It's not easy living with one's mother."

"And your mother is a bit of a spitfire."

"Maybe it's genetic," Renee said and laughed.

"About Collin," Kate said, reaching for another sandwich, "and the way you met . . ."

Renee brightened considerably. It was obviously her favorite subject. "You've read Livvy's articles, so you know the gist of it."

Kate nodded. "It's like something out of a movie."

"It was awfully cute the way he found me."

"Found?"

Renee nodded. "It seemed that way."

"What do you mean?"

"Someone told me later that before we met, they saw him walking along the line of tour buses that were parked near the shopping triangle. It was as if he was looking for something . . . or someone."

Another dot connected. "Really," Kate said. "Did he ever say what he was looking for?"

"He said he was looking for his lost soul mate—me." She paused. "Then later, he told me he was just idly reading where the tour buses were from." She leaned forward. "And believe me, their signs touted groups from all over the world."

"Your coach had a tour sign on it?"

"Of course. The people on the tour have to have a way of identifying it when they return from sightseeing or shopping. We had big fancy magnetic signs on both sides that announced Tennesseans Tour Tuscany."

Bingo. "So Collin knew you were from the US, even Tennessee, before you met him?" Immediately, Kate made note of that fact, though she couldn't yet connect that particular dot to the rest.

"Well, he may not have known I was on that particular coach, but I suppose he might have noticed me when I got off to shop."

Kate's mind was racing. Why would Collin pinpoint a tour group from Tennessee? Or had he been watching for any group from the United States? Either way, if the meeting was planned, Collin could have tailed her through the maze of shops and waited for the chance to bump into her. The cloudburst was perhaps a bit of good fortune, giving him reason to come to her aid like a gallant knight of old with a sweep of his cape and elegant umbrella. He even called her his lady.

"When he said he was traveling the same route, was that before he knew which tour you were on?"

Renee blushed again. "Actually, we decided that together once we both felt the electricity between us. We really didn't want to be separated. He'd rented a car while he was in Italy, and since our tour was completely booked and our coach full, he followed us along our entire route." She sighed happily. "It was heaven until the day we had to say good-bye."

Kate gave her a gentle smile. She didn't want to tell Renee her concerns about the urn or about Collin. At least not until she knew more.

As she helped Renee clear the luncheon dishes and carry them back into the kitchen, she thought how devastating it would be for Renee to find out she was being used, to find out that Collin's affection wasn't genuine.

Then there was the mystery of the urn itself and its real value. She made a mental note to check her e-mail the minute she got home. She couldn't understand why she hadn't heard from Dr. Hosea—unless he had suddenly fallen ill or had been called out of town.

KATE HAD JUST WALKED in the door at home when the phone rang. She ran to the kitchen to pick it up.

It was Melissa. "Mom, we really need your prayers."

"You've got them, honey. Has there been a change?" She was almost afraid to ask.

"Nothing yet. The pediatric cardiologist was here for most of the morning and recommended more tests." She gave Kate the details. "But it's waiting for the results that's so hard. That and thinking about our baby having surgery."

"I have a verse for you, honey," she said. "One with an image you can hold dear through all this." She could hear sniffling on the other end of the phone line. "It's this: 'He tends his flock like a shepherd: He gathers the lambs in his arms and carries them close to his heart; he gently leads those that have young.' That's you, sweetheart," she said, "and John that he's gently leading."

"And it's Mia, too, that he's carrying close to his heart," Melissa added softly. After a moment, she said, "Thank you, Mama."

Melissa hadn't called her that in years. Just the sound of the word brought tears to Kate's eyes.

Chapter Seventeen

As dawn crept through the bedroom window, Kate woke with a start. Through much of the night, she had tossed and turned and fluffed her pillow, only to toss and turn and fluff again. Mostly Melissa, John, and Mia occupied her thoughts, but she also spent some staring-at-the-ceiling time trying to figure out the mystery of the urn, only to keep circling back to her concerns that Renee's Collin was involved in the museum heist in Oxford.

She didn't want to consider it for Renee's sake, but he seemed to be at the center of the dots she'd already connected. If she was right. And that was a big if.

Without disturbing Paul, she grabbed her robe and slipped it on as she padded down the hall to put on the coffee.

She mulled over her nighttime conclusions as she ground the beans.

Collin obviously sought out Renee, possibly because she was with a tour from the United States, perhaps even because she was from Tennessee. He sized her up as a shopper, which was probably not difficult to do: her bright clothing, jewelry, and flamboyant accessories were eye-catching. Plus, a few minutes of observing Renee in any shop would tell even the dullest sleuth that "born to shop" was one of her personal mantras.

A museum piece matching the description of Renee's urn was stolen from a museum in Oxford, conveniently close to Collin's hometown.

In Florence, he talked Renee into purchasing a "similar" piece of ancient art. Was it one and the same?

Her suspicions about him grew, and she shivered, wondering what Renee had gotten herself into.

She poured the fresh grounds into the paper filter, added cold water, and flipped the toggle to turn on the coffeemaker.

If the urn was the real McCoy, it was priceless. How better to get it out of the country than to arrange for some unsuspecting tourist to carry it home packed as a souvenir?

She leaned against the counter, arms crossed.

He was coming to visit Renee under the guise of his affection, even to the point of asking her to marry him. Kate thought about the glow on Renee's face every time she said his name, and Kate's heart ached for her friend.

Still, there were some disconnects. How did the urn get from the museum in Oxford to Florence, Italy? And why was it taken there?

Was there a connection between the Carrot-top and Curly duo, who seemed interested in stealing the urn? Or were they simply out to make a quick buck after reading about the urn in the paper?

Another disconnect: the *Chronicle* said nothing about the urn being more than a copy of an ancient piece. It would then be of no great value to the duo, unless they knew more about it than was mentioned in Livvy's article. And if they did know its real value, how did they? Who told them?

Who was the boss they mentioned?

Could it be Collin Wellington? She pictured Curly and Carrot-top rumbling down Main Street in their GTO, then thought of Renee's description of Collin, from his upper-class British demeanor down to his expertise on everything from antiquities to making a "real" cup of English tea . The professor and the duo in the moonshine car sure didn't appear to make a believable team. But, then, maybe that was precisely the point.

Was it too much of a coincidence that the duo had turned up in town just before Collin had told Renee that he planned to visit her?

She put the dots together in a likely pattern: Collin was in on the heist from the Oxford museum; the "hot" urn was speedily taken from England to Italy; Collin then prearranged for a shop owner who probably owed him some favors to sell the original as a copy to the unwitting Renee; she brought the stolen urn into the United States; Collin Wellington and his gang plan to steal it back again and sell it through the underground to someone with a private collection of such antiquities. Was a tour from Tennessee chosen precisely because the man at the top—the collector—lived there?

The coffee stopped its brew cycle, but Kate barely noticed. She was too busy trying to wrap her mind around the scenario she'd just laid out.

Then a new thought flew into her brain: Why would Collin insist on all the attention with photographs and articles? That didn't make sense if he was trying to fly under the radar.

She poured her coffee and sighed.

It made no sense at all.

KATE HAD JUST FINISHED her quiet time of Bible reading and prayer when Paul shuffled around the corner in his robe and slippers. He grinned at her as he headed to the kitchen, then returned with a cup of coffee and the carafe to refill her mug.

He sat down on the sofa. "You had a bad night?"

"I hoped I wasn't keeping you awake."

"I was awake anyway."

She nodded, knowing that nestled deep into their hearts and minds was the image of a tiny little girl they loved.

"I hope we find out something definitive today," Paul said.

"Melissa said she would call as soon as they hear anything. I'll be in and out today, so I told her to try my cell if they can't get anyone here."

Paul took a sip of coffee. "Good thinking. I've got some early morning meetings at church and a couple of appointments out of the office, so I'll be in and out as well."

Kate couldn't help but wonder what the appointments out of the office were all about, but she bit her tongue and strained to keep her promise to trust Paul. It was so difficult, especially since they'd usually been so open with each other, sharing readily their plans and activities.

She prayed silently, *Lord, give me patience . . . and love.*

"How about you?" Paul asked. "More sleuthing?"

She shrugged. "I've just about given up on the elusive Dr. Hosea. Still no e-mail from him. I'm thinking about contacting some other experts, maybe through one of the university Web sites." She leaned forward intently. "The clock is ticking. According to Renee, Collin will be hopping across the pond before the end of the month. Her emotions are building, and I'm concerned she's being set up for a huge emotional fall. I have to find out if—or maybe I should say *how*—he is connected to all this."

"You don't think she'll figure this out on her own, once he gets here, I mean?"

"You have a point." Kate paused, thinking about the story Renee told her about her background. "But with the heartaches she's endured, I don't want to see her go through another."

PAUL LEFT FOR HIS FIRST MEETING, and Kate showered and dressed for her day, then she headed to the computer to check her e-mail.

She sat back and waited for the slow connection to bring up her e-mail program. Finally, the program loaded onto the computer, and the tiny icon in the bottom corner of her screen showed that she had mail.

She clicked on the icon, and her program opened. The first post was from Dr. Hosea. At last!

Dear Mrs. Hanlon,

I am so sorry for the delay getting back to you. I was unexpectedly called out of town and have just now arrived home. Please call me at your earliest convenience at the number below. I am still extremely interested in the urn.

Sincerely,
Reginald Hosea, PhD

Kate wasted no time trotting to the kitchen and picking up the phone.

The phone showed that she had missed a call, probably while she was in the shower.

Perhaps it was Dr. Hosea, she reasoned, since she had given him her phone number earlier.

But when she pressed the button to listen to the message, the recording of a woman's voice caught her by surprise. Even more alarming was the message.

"You need to wire an additional three thousand dollars," the crisp, professional voice said, "in order to bring your account up to date. This must be done by the twentieth of the month, otherwise . . ." the voice cut out. It sounded like the caller was on a cell phone that had lost its signal.

Kate fell into a chair at the kitchen table, stunned by what she'd just heard. *Another three thousand dollars?* Their budget had been too tight to allow for a trip to Italy. Now this? What kind of financial trap were they caught in?

Chapter Eighteen

Kate was still in shock over the voice-mail message about the money when she dialed Dr. Hosea. She tried to push it from her mind as she waited for him to pick up.

He finally answered on the fourth ring. Again he apologized for not getting back to her. He was professional, yet surprisingly warm and cordial as they spoke, and when she suggested he travel to Copper Mill from southern Tennessee to examine the urn in person, he readily agreed. Kate bit back her disappointment when he said he was booked for a couple of weeks. Then after a moment's pause, he added, "Though if I can rearrange some appointments and meetings, perhaps I can come up tomorrow."

Kate let out a pent-up sigh of relief. "That would be great." She started to give him directions to Faith Briar.

He surprised her by saying, "No need. I already know where it is." Before Kate could react to that curious news, he laughed and added, "My GPS. I never leave home without it."

WEDNESDAY MORNING, just before ten o'clock, Kate turned the Honda into the parking lot at Faith Briar. At the same time, a nondescript minivan approached from the opposite direction and pulled in to park beside her.

She exited her car and waited as a rumpled-appearing man with a round face and rather unkempt beard got out of the minivan. He wore khakis and a plaid shirt, sleeves rolled midforearm, and an Indiana Jones hat. Central casting couldn't have chosen a better look for an archaeologist.

Kate couldn't help smiling. "Dr. Hosea?"

He assessed her with piercing blue-gray eyes and an engaging smile. "Yes, and you must be Mrs. Hanlon."

"Please, call me Kate."

"Well, thank you, Kate. And please call me Reg." He laughed heartily. "Reg as in 'I *pledge*' to present you with the best information possible about this interesting urn that's landed in Copper Mill, Tennessee." His accent was intriguing. A bit Southern, a bit British, or possibly Australian.

He rounded the van, opened the sliding side door and reached inside. When he came back around where Kate was standing, he was carrying a worn leather satchel, the size and shape of a pilot's flight bag. "All right, then. I'm ready."

As they headed toward the church, Kate said, "Oh, and Dr. Hosea, I'd appreciate your discretion, because I haven't yet told the owner about the urn's potential value."

He raised a bushy brow. "I'm quite aware you mean Renee Lambert. And I'm assuming you've also not told her it might have been stolen?"

Kate drew in a sharp breath. "You know about that?"

"Oh yes, of course." He paused when they reached the church entrance. "I've been following the reports very closely." He held the door open for Kate, and she stepped through.

The spotlight in the glass case cast an ethereal glow on the urn, and Kate noticed that Reg was as taken by it as she had been. Perhaps even more, judging from his expression.

Kate excused herself momentarily to go to Millie's office to get the key, while Reg set his satchel on the floor by the case.

"May I?" Reg shot Kate a questioning look after she opened the door.

"Of course. You can remove it from the case if you'd like."

Instead of removing it, however, he cautiously touched the urn. His expression told Kate that he took great pleasure in his work. Without removing the urn, he turned it slightly to the right, inspected it closely, then continued to turn it a fraction of an inch at a time until he had studied the relief art on the two longer sides as well as on each end beneath the cherubim guardians. He moved the piece, touching the figures of Francis and Clare with his fingertips, as if assessing how they might have been carved. Or perhaps *if* they had been carved, which she wondered might indicate the urn's age.

He turned to the satchel, clicked it open, and then pulled out a small folding table and set it up with a snap. Next, he put together a telescoping stand, attached a spotlight, and arranged it so that it brightly illuminated the table. Kate spotted various containers at the bottom of the satchel, and a separate open compartment containing tools and brushes. She was impressed with the array of testing materials.

Finally, Reg covered the small table with a thick padded top that appeared to be made of black felt.

"Now, let's see what we've got," he breathed as he went back to the glass case.

He lifted the urn from its glass shelf and, moving slowly, placed it on the table, adjusted the light, and then picked up a magnifying glass.

"What do you make of the symbols?" Kate asked. "They strike me as odd."

"They are unique, and not many people can interpret them. But after studying the photographs you sent, and now that I see the urn, I've identified at least some of the symbols and have translated a portion of the writings."

"Does it tell the story of Francis and Clare, their relationship, I mean?"

"That's exactly what it tells, though not in detail, of course." He turned to look up at her. "No one knows the true story."

For a half hour, Reg remained bent over the urn. He seldom spoke but kept working in a rhythmic fashion as if he'd done this thing dozens, if not hundreds, of times. Every few minutes he reached for a different tool or brush, opened a bottle of this or a jar of that, applied a minute dab of chemical or powder, then sat back as if to watch some sort of reaction from the alabaster that Kate couldn't see.

Kate gave him plenty of room to work so he wouldn't feel like she was breathing down his neck. She was particularly curious to see if he would try to open the urn by pressing on the cherubim and wondered if he knew about the secret steps to opening the urn.

Finally, he sat back and shot her a pleased look. "This is preliminary, of course, and we can't know without further testing if it's the crematory urn missing from the Exeter. At this point, I can't even tell you the age. Of course, I can give you some parameters, but not anything substantive.

"I would like to take it with me, with your permission, of course, to run a more thorough test. I believe it's simply a good copy, but we can't know for certain."

"I don't know if that's possible. We would need to get Mrs. Lambert's permission," Kate said. "And knowing her, I really doubt she'd let it go."

Just then, Paul opened the door between the foyer and the church offices and looked in. "How's it going?"

Reg glanced up from his work and gave Paul a nod. Kate thought she saw a shadow of irritation.

It disappeared when she said, "Reg, this is my husband, Pastor Paul Hanlon."

"Oh, I didn't realize you were the minister's wife," Reg said. He stood and shook Paul's hand.

"One and the same," Kate said.

"How did you get involved with the details of the urn?"

"Kate's an amateur sleuth." Paul shot her a proud smile.

"And Collin Wellington is a friend of mine."

A lightbulb went on in Kate's head. "Do you know Collin?"

Reg laughed. "Everyone who's anyone in our related fields knows the great Sir Wellington."

Kate gasped. "*Sir* Wellington?"

Reg laughed. "In his dreams. He's been after the Queen to

bestow knighthood on him for years. It's no secret. Actually, he'd be the first to admit it."

Reg began putting his satchel back together. "I was just telling your wife that until I do further testing, and other experts have a look at the urn, we really don't know much more than when I arrived. So far it appears to be an incredibly clever copy."

"Is Collin Wellington trustworthy in your opinion?" Kate asked as Reg returned the urn to the glass shelf.

He adjusted it slightly so the spotlight illumined it with the glow that seemed to emanate from inside, then turned back to Kate. "Why do you ask?"

"Just curious, I suppose," she said quickly.

He didn't answer right away, then furrowing his brow, he said, "His reputation is spotless in his field. But there have been rumors lately about him getting himself into some sort of financial difficulty." He paused. "I take it you're asking because of the romance between your friend and Wellington. I don't like to pass along hearsay, but in this case, I believe it's warranted. If I were you, I would advise her to go slowly, get to know him well before making any commitment. You never know what a person might do when he's got money troubles."

Kate exchanged glances with Paul, who raised an eyebrow. "Thank you for your honesty," she said to Reg after a brief hesitation.

"When I read the story in your *Chronicle* about how they met, I wondered about its coincidence," he said.

"So did we," Kate said.

"Well, folks, it's been good to meet you." He reached out

to shake Kate's hand, then Paul's. "I hope you understand that I have to report this to the FBI. I believe what you have here is a copy, a very good one, but the uncertainty of my preliminary findings, plus the museum robberies, make it necessary."

"Does that mean they'll be coming for it?" Paul asked.

"I really don't know. I don't work closely with them. I'm just required to report findings such as this. However, I will be letting them know about today's tests. They may well require you to give up the piece for further testing." He shrugged. "I really can't say."

He said his good-byes, wished them luck, then with satchel in hand, he headed back to the minivan. Kate and Paul stood at the entrance of the church, watching him cross the parking lot. Before he reached his vehicle, he was in deep conversation on his cell phone.

Kate sighed. "We really don't know much more about the urn than we did before he got here."

"I know you're disappointed."

She smiled. "It's true I was expecting an easy end to at least part of the mystery of the urn's origins. I just had the feeling he wasn't telling me everything he knows about the urn."

"How did you pick up on that?"

She considered the question as she watched Reg climb into his vehicle. "More from what he didn't say than what he did say. And the FBI comment. If there was any doubt that this wasn't a copy, don't you think he'd have them over here before we could say Rumpelstiltskin?" She thought about it for a moment. "Perhaps even have brought an agent with him?"

Her husband laughed and circled his arm around her

shoulders. They waved as the archaeologist, Indiana Jones hat pulled low over his forehead, drove off in the minivan.

"That's another thing I love about you."

She wrinkled her nose, looking up at him. "What?"

"The hypotheses you toss in my direction when you're sleuthing. You keep my brain doing calisthenics."

"By the way," she said. The voice message concerning the thousands of dollars they owed weighed heavily on her mind. But as she looked into his eyes, she didn't want to break her promise, or see that sparkle of fun and love disappear, so she just smiled and gave him a quick kiss before trotting to her car.

As she pulled out of the parking lot and turned right on Mountain Laurel, she spotted Reg's van and hurried to catch up with it.

She wasn't intending to tail him, but when it came time for her to turn onto Smoky Mountain Road, she decided against it and followed him into town.

He parked right in front of the diner. Nothing unusual in that. Except when she slowed to pull to the side of the road, she saw the GTO in the nearby library parking lot.

Her heart slammed into her ribs. Could there be a connection between Dr. Hosea and the Carrot-top and Curly duo?

She got out of the car and hesitated, wondering if she should look around inside the diner or wait to see who might emerge.

But before she could decide, the door of the diner opened, and the Diner Duo waltzed out, arguing about who was going to drive.

Seconds later, Reg exited with a takeout bag and a Styrofoam cup.

Reg didn't even give so much as a glance toward the GTO as it revved its engine and roared down the street.

But before the car disappeared, Curly, who was in the passenger seat, turned and looked back.

And it appeared he was looking straight at Reg.

Chapter Nineteen

Thursday afternoon, Kate sat at the kitchen table to read Livvy's latest article in that morning's edition of the *Chronicle*. The sting of tears came again as she read about Livvy's impressions of her two days in Assisi.

Joys Discovered in Assisi
by Livvy Jenner

The tolling bells from the Basilica of Santa Chiara gently woke me on our first morning in Assisi. I got out of bed and walked to the window, which I had left open the night before. The evening breeze had quickly lulled me to sleep.

As I approached the window, my breath was taken away. Directly in front of me, I could see the city of Assisi beginning to come to life as the sun crept up in the sky. I tried to count the number of church towers and stopped at about sixteen. So many other things were craving my attention.

I looked to my left and saw the early morning mist beginning to rise, revealing the olive groves rolling down the hillside from Assisi toward San Damiano. I was so enthralled I could hardly move. But when I glanced at the alarm clock, I realized that breakfast would be served in twenty minutes, and I needed to get ready.

Kate got up to pour herself a glass of iced tea as she struggled to get her emotions under control. *I know it was in our best interest not to go. But how I miss realizing that dream.* She sat back down and picked up the paper again.

After breakfast, the tour's first excursion was to the Basilica of San Francesco. The basilica was less than a mile away from the hotel, so walking was in order—though not your ordinary morning stroll, to be sure. Assisi is built on a hillside, so every street goes either uphill or downhill. And they are narrow cobblestone streets with sidewalks barely wide enough for one person.

The ubiquitous coffee shops—or coffee bars, as they're called—sent forth the wonderful aroma of coffee and freshly baked bread as we made our way across town.

The article continued with descriptions of their visits to several sites of interest in the city of Assisi, ending with a side trip to the Carceri at Mount Subasio, where Francis and his followers often went to get away and pray.

Kate folded the newspaper and placed it on the counter so Paul could read it when he got home. The phone rang, and she hurried toward it, hoping it was Melissa.

It was Renee.

Renee's voice took on the excited pitch of a much younger woman's. "I just had the most wonderful news," she breathed into the telephone. She rushed on, not waiting for Kate to respond. "It's about Collin. He called this morning to tell me he was on his way to Heathrow."

"To fly here?"

"Where else?"

"That's wonderful, Renee. We can't wait to meet him." That was an understatement.

"And meet him you shall! That's why I called," she said. "I'm inviting a few friends over for a little welcome tea in honor of him tomorrow afternoon. I would like for you and Paul to attend."

"I'll check with Paul, but I think our calendar's clear." As mysterious as Paul's behavior had been lately, she couldn't be sure of where he would be when.

"Collin is staying at the Hamilton Springs Hotel."

Kate wondered what she was getting at. "*Mmm*, that's nice. It's the loveliest place in town."

"I'm telling you that so if anyone asks, you can assure them he's not moving in here with Mother and me."

"Oh, I don't think anyone—"

"After the rumors that Mother's been spreading all over town, don't be surprised if it comes up in conversation."

Kate sighed. "I'll be glad to let people know."

"Good. Four o'clock, then, tomorrow for afternoon tea."

"I wouldn't miss it." She wondered at the shiver that traveled up her spine, though, as she replaced the phone in the receiver.

Of course, she wouldn't miss the tea—for Renee's sake. But something told her there might be more than social niceties exchanged.

She shivered again.

Chapter Twenty

Kate and Paul arrived at Renee's home at a quarter to four. It was a perfect day for a tea—sunny and breezy with a scattering of buttermilk clouds to keep the air cool—and Kate was glad for Renee's sake.

A beaming Renee met them at the door. Collin was at her side, looking every bit the English gentleman. Again, Kate was reminded of Anthony Hopkins in *Shadowlands*.

He smiled at Kate as Renee introduced them, bent to kiss her hand, then gave Paul a hearty handshake.

He was charming. Kate could think of no better word to describe him during the first few minutes after they met. She could see why Renee was smitten with him.

After they stepped inside, Renee excused herself to see to things in the kitchen, and Collin, acting as if he were already the gentleman of the house, escorted Kate and Paul out to the back patio and flower garden.

Kate caught her breath. The setting was even prettier than the day Renee had invited her to lunch. There were three round tables set with linens of different shades of pink.

A floral teapot had been placed in the center of each table beside a small vase of violets, pink roses, and baby's breath.

Those who had arrived before Paul and Kate were milling about the garden sipping sparkling drinks in glass flutes, each with a floating strawberry.

"Would you care for some sparkling cider?" Collin asked Kate. His earlier warmth seemed to cool before her eyes and she shivered.

She didn't like the way his eyes seemed to pierce hers or his frosty scrutiny as he assessed her. But for appearances, she smiled and said, "Yes, that would be lovely. Thank you."

"And you, Reverend Hanlon?"

"I'll take a glass, but let me help you," Paul said, and the two walked over to another round table on the patio that held the bottles of cider, silver service for tea and coffee, and some small crystal bowls of mints and mixed nuts.

Kate spotted Caroline sitting off to one side of the garden, her expression sour. Kisses sat on her lap, and his expression was equally perturbed. He seemed to be staring directly at Collin, who was filling the flutes.

Kate made her way over to Caroline and pulled up a folding chair.

"The least she could've done was invite some of my friends," Caroline grumbled.

Kate glanced around. "Renee told me she planned to invite the Copper Mill folks who met Collin on the tour. I'm sure she did it to put Collin at ease. I think it's a lovely gesture."

"*Hmmph,*" Caroline said. "You, your husband, and me are the obvious exceptions. So much for putting us at ease."

Kisses put his ears back and growled as Collin and Paul walked over with the sparkling-cider flutes. And it wasn't Paul he was growling at.

Collin didn't seem to notice. He handed Kate her drink, then smiled at Caroline. "Mrs. Johnston, may I get you something to drink?" The rumbling growl from the little Chihuahua grew louder.

"I told you," she said, "that kind of cider doesn't agree with me."

"Ah yes, so you did," he said, never losing his smile. "How about something else? Perhaps a glass of milk might settle the stomach." His British upper-class accent made even an ordinary glass of milk sound elegant.

Caroline sniffed. "I wouldn't care for anything, thank you." Another menacing growl from Kisses accentuated her words.

Mayor Lawton Briddle and his wife, Lucy Mae, walked over to join them, breaking the awkward moment. And just then, Livvy and Danny Jenner arrived and made a beeline over to greet Collin. LuAnne was next, livening the party considerably with her noisy arrival and shout of "*Buon giorno!*" when she spotted Collin. She almost knocked him over with a giant bear hug.

Through it all, Collin seemed to be taking the friendly adulation with good humor. There was no hint of the stiff British countenance Kate had expected.

When the hubbub died down, Collin said to Livvy, who was standing between him and Kate, "Your articles have been wonderfully written."

Livvy flushed. "Thank you. I'm pleased you came up with the idea. We've had a lot of interest in the urn. A steady stream of visitors have come to see its display at the church, even folks from out of town."

"I'm looking forward to seeing it again myself," Collin said and lifted his flute to his lips.

In that instant, Kate thought she caught a glint of warning in his eyes as he met her gaze over the rim of the flute. If she'd blinked, she would have missed it.

Stunned, she watched him carefully as he turned to chat with those who'd been on the Triple T Tour. They drifted off to one side, sharing memories and laughter and chatter about putting together another trip somewhere else in the world.

Paul gave Kate an understanding squeeze of the fingers as Livvy left the others and returned to Kate's side.

"Forgive us," she said. "This has turned into a reunion that I don't really think Renee intended."

"Nothing to forgive, really." Kate looked around. "But speaking of Renee, I haven't seen her since we got here. Maybe we should go in and see if we can help."

"Good idea," Livvy said, and the two left for the kitchen.

They found Renee putting the final touches on three tiered dishes of finger sandwiches.

"Let us carry these out for you," Kate said, reaching for one of the dishes.

When Renee met her gaze, Kate could see a spark of fiery emotion in her eyes.

"Is everything okay?"

"Of course," Renee huffed. "If you don't consider the war Mother has declared."

"Oh dear," Kate said.

"Not only that. She's got an ally."

Livvy had stepped up to take another of the sandwich plates. "Who is that?"

Renee shook her head. "The last creature I would have expected it from. Kisses."

"Collin is a charming man," Kate said. "I'm sure he'll win them over in time."

Renee's penciled brow arched. "Not necessarily. I just found out Collin detests small dogs." Then her expression softened. "But he did say that he'd do anything for me, including learning to love a dog that reminds him of a rodent."

Rodent? If anyone else on the planet had dared to compare Kisses to a rodent, Renee would have been up in arms. It appeared Collin had truly won her heart.

The party went on without a hitch. Even Caroline seemed to loosen up and have a good time. When Collin fixed her a special cup of tea and a scone with Devonshire cream he'd brought from England, she actually gave him a begrudging smile—right before telling him she thought it had curdled during its transatlantic flight.

WHILE THE MEAL was being served, Kate leaned back in her chair and met the probing gaze of the man who'd been seated across from her: Collin Wellington. Renee sat to his right, and Paul sat to Kate's. Their conversation had been pleasant, but when Kate brought up Collin's academic background and interests, he had successfully evaded every direct question.

Finally, she put down her scone and leaned forward. "I'd love to know more about the urn," she said pleasantly.

His smile seemed to tighten. "What more is there to know?

It's a beautiful replica, and I think Renee made a wise decision when she purchased it."

"I'm curious about how the urn opens," Kate said. "She said you demonstrated how it's done when she first bought it, but she hasn't been able to open it since. She showed me the steps, but I couldn't do it either."

His smile seemed plastered in place, and his eyes were growing cooler by the second. "It's tricky," he said evenly. "I'll have to show her again. And you, if you would like."

"Yes, you will, dear," Renee said, beaming up at him.

"And the language is a curiosity," Kate went on. "Etruscan."

Collin's eyes widened. "You're very observant."

Beside her, Paul chuckled. "If you knew my Kate better, you'd know that's an understatement."

"Is that a fact?" Collin said, his eyes never leaving Kate's.

"I'm just so curious about it. It seems interesting that the artist would use a thousand-year-old language paired with artwork depicting Saint Francis and Saint Clare."

"That's what makes the original so valuable. It's quite an unusual piece because the artist, back in the twelfth century, wanted to honor both Saint Francis and the history of the language of the area."

"And the original is . . . ?" Kate asked, lifting her brow.

He colored slightly and looked away from Kate's probing gaze. "We'll leave that subject for another time." His expression emphasized the conversation was over.

Around them rose the sounds of laughter and light banter as the other guests talked about their memories.

Kate stood. "I'll clear the dishes," she said to Renee.

Paul started to stand to help her, but Collin insisted he sit down and said he would give her a hand. A smiling Renee looked on with approval.

Kate bustled into the kitchen, carrying two empty tiered sandwich plates, one in each hand. Collin was a few steps behind her.

He surprised her by closing the door behind them as they stepped inside. She placed the dishes on the counter and turned to look at him.

This time there was no mistaking the warning in his eyes. "Follow me," he said in a clipped tone.

She blinked and didn't argue, but her heart pounded in alarm.

He led her into the living room, glanced around to make sure no one was near; then stepped menacingly close. "I understand you made an online inquiry about me."

There was nothing charming about his accent now.

Kate backed away from him. "Not about you. About your writing."

"Specifically, about my papers having to do with ancient urns such as the souvenir Renee brought home with her." His eyes glittered and his cool expression turned colder still as he moved closer to Kate. "Stay out of this. You have no idea what you're getting into."

Kate swallowed hard and blinked again. She tried to find her voice to tell him he had no right to tell her what to do or not do, but only a squeak came out.

"Consider this a warning," he said. Then turning abruptly, he disappeared back into the kitchen.

Chapter Twenty-One

Kate's knees were still shaking when she heard Collin return to Renee and the others outside, his charm once again in place, his banter as lively as the others'.

Taking a deep cleansing breath, Kate followed. As she sat down next to Paul, he said, "You look like you've seen a ghost."

Across the table, Collin's gaze was on her, and though he wore a smile of concern that matched Renee's and Paul's, his piercing eyes were as cold as ice.

Kate shivered. "I'm suddenly not feeling so well. I think we'd better go," she said to Paul.

As they drove home, she told Paul about Collin's warning to stay out of things. The memory of his cold eyes, his harsh expression, and his unpleasant tone made a shiver creep up her back.

Paul glanced across the car at her, his lips in a thin line. "You should have told me right away," he said. "He had no right to speak to you in such a way—especially when you were alone."

Kate drew in a deep breath. "I never felt I was in any real danger. Otherwise, I would have." She reached for his hand. "Honest."

Though her words were brave and meant to reassure Paul, Kate had to admit there was something about Collin that made her more than wary. She was afraid of him. Flat out afraid. She shivered again, wondering what she had gotten herself into.

THAT NIGHT, long after Paul fell asleep, Kate lay awake.

She couldn't get Collin out of her mind, or the voice mail demanding three thousand dollars. *What on earth can that be about?*

Different scenarios kept running through her head. If Paul didn't have a serious medical problem that he hadn't told her about, was someone blackmailing him? The thought was ludicrous, but in the dark of the night, it flitted through her mind and left her wondering. Maybe some huge debt had come due that she didn't know anything about.

But she and Paul always shared this kind of information. To keep it from her was so unlike him.

Then her thoughts turned to Mia, still in the hospital, the doctors still running tests. How much more uncertainty could she take? So much troubled her that night. It was even difficult for her to quiet her heart before the Lord and pray before going to sleep.

Usually, during her quiet moments of prayer, even after the most disturbing day, her heart was filled with peace.

But this night was different.

There were other niggling concerns stirring her brain cells and keeping her wide awake long after bedtime.

She drew in a shaky breath, again remembering the look on Collin's face when he threatened her. Should she tell Renee about this other side of the man she'd fallen in love with?

But what did Kate know about him exactly? Was it enough to upset Renee with her worries about Collin?

Staring at the ceiling, she finally decided she would wait to tell Renee once she figured out what Wellington was hiding and how he fit into the mystery of the urn. For now, she promised herself she would leave no stone unturned while following leads, no matter the danger.

Unable to sleep, she decided it was time for a review. She headed into the kitchen for the pencil and pad, then returned to the living room. A few minutes later, she started jotting down what she knew about the case:

1. Collin helped Renee pick out a souvenir urn to bring home with her to the States.

2. The urn is similar, if not identical, to one that was stolen nine months ago near where Collin lives in Oxford.

3. Seven other museum heists had occurred worldwide in the last nine months. The FBI and Scotland Yard had teamed up to catch the thieves.

4. Dr. Hosea said he couldn't determine the age of the urn, despite the tests he ran, but he believes it's probably a copy. Or does he really?

Question: why didn't he comment on the Etruscan

language and thousand-year difference between language symbols and relief art of Saint Francis?

Consideration: maybe he did notice these things and didn't think them important enough to mention.

5. Dr. Hosea wanted to take the urn with him for further testing.

Question: if there was even a hint that the urn was authentic, wouldn't he have insisted that it be kept under lock and key until the FBI, Scotland Yard, and/or local authorities arrived to take possession?

6. Collin arrived in town ahead of schedule. He said, "You have no idea what you're getting into." Yet how did he know she was getting into anything? The only thing that could have gotten back to him was her inquiry about the published papers. Unless he was involved with the Diner Duo and/or Dr. Hosea.

All this made her head hurt. She sat back in the rocker and stared at the list, her gaze lingering on Collin's name. One thing for sure, he was a major player and somehow involved in at least the heist from the Exeter Museum of Art and Antiquities. Now that Collin was here in Copper Mill, did that mean another heist was about to go down? Right in front of their noses . . . at Faith Briar?

If so, that meant the urn was authentic and of enormous value. And Renee had been duped into carrying a piece of ancient art into the country illegally.

It was an ingenious plan; she had to give Collin credit for that. He dupes Renee into buying the stolen urn so it can be transported into the country without suspicion. He arrives to take it into his possession, then rides off into the sunset, never to be heard from again.

An international fugitive who leaves Renee with a broken heart.

Kate pondered that sad thought for a moment, then another thought grabbed her brain and wouldn't let go: if she *had* correctly identified all the puzzle pieces, why didn't they fit together?

What was missing?

Chapter Twenty-Two

Saturday morning, Kate straightened up the house in anticipation of John and Melissa bringing Mia home from the hospital. Then she sat at the table and made out a grocery list for a trip to the Mercantile, choosing ingredients for their favorite meals.

John loved Paul's famous chili, and Melissa had always favored Kate's lemon-meringue pie above all other desserts. And, of course, Mia's favorite food of recent days was blue pancakes. She would work all three into the next few days' menus. She scanned the pantry cupboard for the needed ingredients, tucked the list in her handbag, and headed to the car.

She had just crossed Smoky Mountain Road on her way to the Mercantile when she spotted an approaching car, a dark BMW, being driven by someone who, at first glance, looked like Collin.

She slowed the Honda and watched in her rearview mirror as the vehicle turned east on Mountain Laurel Road, then disappeared from sight.

Could it have been Collin? There had been a dark BMW parked in front of Renee's house the day before, but Kate hadn't thought to ask if it was his. Curiosity got the best of her, so she pulled into the lot next to Copper Mill Park and turned the Honda around. She drove back to the intersection where she'd seen the BMW and squinted east. There wasn't a car in sight.

She turned east on Mountain Laurel and drove slowly, peering across fields and lots.

Nothing.

Faith Briar was now on her left, and she slowed and turned into the parking lot. It was empty, just as it was on most Saturdays. She circled the lot, examining the shrubs and stands of pines, hemlocks, and small oaks that bordered it.

Nothing.

As she headed toward the exit, a glint of metal caught her eye, and she pressed on the brake. There, behind the church, almost hidden behind some heavy undergrowth and woody vines, was a dark, sleek metallic object. A car. Probably the BMW.

And most probably Collin.

She exited the lot and parked on the street several yards from Faith Briar, then hurried to the back entrance of the church.

Her knees were shaking and she tried not to think of Collin's piercingly cold eyes when he told her to mind her own business. She felt her pocket for her cell phone, realizing too late that she'd left it home.

Then again, what would she say if she did call the sheriff? At this point, she had no evidence that Collin had done anything wrong. She supposed she could accuse him of breaking and entering, but even that scenario was iffy. He'd probably let himself in with Renee's key.

Besides, shaky knees or not, she preferred catching him red-handed if he'd come to reclaim "his" urn.

She pulled Paul's key out of her pocket, let herself in without a sound, then slipped into the sanctuary and crept silently down the aisle toward the foyer. When she reached the double doors, she attempted to peer through the crack between them.

She couldn't see anything.

Gingerly, she pushed one door open a few inches and squinted around the small room.

There was no sign of movement, or of anything unusual going on, so she pushed the door open wide enough to slip through.

The door of the glass case housing the urn was wide open. The spotlight was on, but the urn was missing.

And there was no sign of Collin.

He had probably let himself out the front door, she reasoned . . . until she heard footsteps on the stairs leading to the foyer from the church basement.

There was no time to hide or even run back into the sanctuary.

So she waited, her knees threatening to give out at any instant, as the footsteps moved closer.

When Collin opened the door at the top of the stairs, he didn't seem the least bit surprised to see Kate standing by the empty glass case, gaping at him.

He gave her a crisp nod as he brushed past, holding the urn gingerly with both hands. With steady, delicate maneuvering, he returned it to the case and closed the door.

"Does Renee know what you're up to?" Kate asked, once she found her voice again.

He gave her a piercing stare. "No, and I don't expect you to tell her."

"You're using my friend. It will take a lot more than an empty threat to stop me from protecting her." Kate's voice was soft but firm. She hoped it didn't give away how frightened she was of this man.

"Empty threat?" He shook his head. "That was not an empty threat. I warned you for your own good. Stay out of this, or someone will get hurt."

"It's too late for that." She was thinking about Renee. "You've played with the emotions of someone I care about, someone a lot of us care about. You've deceived her for your own purposes; you've put her in danger of arrest—or worse."

He stared at her, unblinking, with those piercing eyes. His voice was almost a growl. "You don't know what you're talking about." He moved toward the door, paused, then looked back at Kate. "Again, I give you warning. Stay away from this. There's going to be trouble, and you're going to find yourself in the middle of it. And then, dear Mrs. Hanlon, you will find it too late to take care of your friend, yourself, or anyone else."

Without another word, he stepped outside. She heard his retreating footsteps.

Kate stared at the back of the closed door for a moment, gathering her thoughts. Suddenly a thought occurred to her.

How did he get the case open? She dashed into Millie's office and found the key exactly where it was supposed to be. Another dot to be connected.

And what was he doing with the urn, anyway? Why would he take it downstairs? The basement contained a multipurpose room, a small kitchen, and two small Sunday-school classrooms. She couldn't think of a reason that made sense.

It took her less than thirty seconds to decide she needed to investigate his actions. She flipped on the stairwell light and hurried down to the basement. She opened the door to the first classroom. It was the nursery, and it looked undisturbed. There was a diaper-changing table where he might have laid the urn while he was working on it, but there was no sign that the table had been used, and none of the cribs appeared to have been disturbed.

The second classroom door was closed, and nothing seemed disturbed in the kitchen or multipurpose room. She headed back upstairs to the foyer. She'd left her handbag on a chair near the entrance to the church office, and as she went over to pick it up, the urn caught her attention.

It seemed undisturbed, though she knew Collin had just returned it. He had been careful to replace it exactly as he had found it. She went to Millie's office, grabbed the key, then opened the case and carefully lifted the urn. The light in the foyer was too dim to see properly, so just as she had done before, she carried it into the sanctuary and sat in a pew by one of the side windows.

Turning it in her lap, she again admired the beauty of the workmanship—the figures of Saint Francis and Saint Clare;

the detail in the symmetry of the composition with the background animals; the expressions on the villagers' faces on the opposite side, depicting Saint Francis and the Wolf of Gubbio. And then there were the cherubim on either end of the urn and the breathtaking detail in their faces.

Sunlight was pouring through the window in such a way that the urn seemed to glow from some inner source, just as she had noticed before. Only this time, it seemed even more pronounced.

She touched the symbols of the ancient language, then she blinked and her heart skipped a beat.

She held the urn closer. The cherubim at the top of the urn had each been turned slightly toward the figures of Saint Francis and Saint Clare. She hadn't known until this moment that they were not stationary.

Renee, following Collin's original instructions, had attempted to show Kate the steps to unlocking the urn: using her thumbs, she'd pressed the crossed bare feet of the two cherubim at the same time.

When Renee tried it, nothing happened. But at that time, Kate realized now, the cherubim had been turned slightly toward the relief of Saint Francis and the Wolf of Gubbio.

Someone had changed the configuration of the urn, and it was obvious who had done it. The question was why? Unless . . .

Holding her breath, Kate pressed her thumbs against the tiny feet of the angels.

The urn clicked open.

Chapter Twenty-Three

Kate placed the urn back in the case and closed the door, her mind whirling with possibilities. She thought again about the basement. It was obvious that Collin had taken the urn downstairs for some reason. If he'd simply wanted to open it, he could have done that in the foyer.

Why would he need extra space, or perhaps privacy, to open the urn? Had he taken something out? Or had he put something in?

She opened the basement door once more and trotted down the stairs.

This time, it was no once-over. She pulled a penlight out of her handbag and, starting in the multipurpose room, got down on hands and knees, checking under tables and chairs. She found a few dust bunnies, but nothing else.

She checked the kitchen counters, looking for anything that might give her a clue. They had been wiped clean. She checked the trash container, but it was empty.

Next, she headed to the classrooms. The first, which served as a nursery, took her some time. She looked under the cribs and changing tables, shining the beam of her flashlight across the floor. Nothing.

Kate opened the door to the second classroom, flipped on the light, and stepped inside. A scattering of brightly colored plastic tables and chairs were strewn about the room. It seemed to Kate like the last place someone would come to open the urn.

She started to leave when something caught her eye. The little trash receptacle was missing its plastic liner. She knew the fresh liners were kept in rolls beneath the old, so she went over to make the replacement.

There, at the bottom of the receptacle, was some sort of strange battery. She reached for it, frowned, and held it up to the light, turning it one way, then the other. Shaped like a small postage stamp, it wasn't like anything she'd ever seen. It certainly wasn't anything that belonged in a Sunday-school classroom.

She tucked it into a tissue, folded the tissue, and put it in the zippered coin section of her wallet.

AS KATE SHOPPED at the Mercantile and later put away her groceries, she tried to make sense of finding Collin at the church with the urn. Why did he take the urn downstairs and then return it to its original place as if undisturbed?

It *was* disturbed. He had opened the urn and either forgot to lock it again or left it open on purpose. Why?

She was in the kitchen getting ready to stir together some corn bread, still pondering her nagging questions, when Paul came in the door. He had the day's mail in hand, a stack of envelopes and ads, and set it on the counter by the telephone.

He came over to give her a quick kiss, then stopped and waggled his eyebrows at the cornmeal mixture. "From scratch?"

She nodded. "Your favorite."

"A perfect accompaniment for the chili. And the sweeter the better." He went to the pantry cupboard and pulled out the sugar canister.

"I already put in one more scoop than the recipe calls for."

He gave her a pleading look that she couldn't resist. She stood back while he added another scoop.

"Have you heard anything from the kids?"

Kate shook her head. They spoke for a few minutes about the latest tests and the difficult waiting period they were all going through. Kate felt herself sag wearily against him. Yes, she was worried about Mia, but also about the financial troubles they were in . . . and the fact that Paul wasn't being straight with her.

Paul's expression was filled with concern as he met her eyes. "We've been under a lot of pressure lately. How about going out for dinner? Maybe it would help to do something special just for the two of us."

She smiled. "Cheeseburgers at the diner? That sounds wonderful."

"I was thinking of the Bristol."

"Oh, Paul, we can't afford that. Especially not now."

He frowned. "We don't do things like this often, Kate. And I really would like to do something to lift your spirits."

She studied the compassion in his face. He really would give her the whole world if he could.

But her concerns about the money they owed, for whatever

reason, strengthened her resolve to say no to any frivolous expenditures.

"Actually, honey, I would prefer the diner." She touched his cheek, thinking about her promise to trust him. She just wished he trusted her with whatever bad news it was that he was keeping from her.

His shoulders sagged, confirming her suspicions. It was indeed bad news.

THEY HAD JUST taken their seats at the Country Diner when the front door opened and Renee, Caroline, and Collin came in. Renee made a beeline to their booth, telling everyone within earshot about the wonderful day she and Collin had spent together as she showed him the sights of Copper Mill.

Collin, ever the polite and debonair gentleman, smiled but avoided meeting Kate's gaze.

"Collin was planning to take me to dinner at the Bristol," Renee said.

Caroline stepped up, tapping her cane with each incremental movement forward. "I told them the food's better here, and if they'd change their minds about the Bristol, I'd join them."

Renee and Collin smiled at each other over Caroline's head. It was a sweet exchange, and Kate had a difficult time reconciling this Collin with the Collin she'd run into at Renee's tea and at Faith Briar.

Paul fell quiet as he studied Collin, probably sensing Kate's distrust of the man. His tight-lipped expression told her he was still upset at how Collin had threatened Kate.

Kate touched his hand, determined to change the direction of their thoughts so they could enjoy dinner. "I've never seen Renee so happy," she said as the threesome moved on to their table. "And did you notice, Kisses isn't with her?"

Paul glanced toward the group. "You're right. Not a sign of him, not even a tote."

"It must be a compromise. It seems the little guy didn't take to Collin right off, and the feeling was mutual."

Paul let out a soft whistle. "Now that could be trouble."

Kate sighed. "Actually, I suspect that Kisses and Collin's relationship will be the least of her troubles."

She told Paul about her encounter with Collin at the church.

Paul worked his jaw as he again glanced across the room at Collin. Then he leaned in closer to Kate. "You had better be cautious in your dealings with him. From everything we know, he's not safe to be around. We still don't know what his role is in this whole caper."

He was also intrigued by the strange battery she'd discovered in the basement, and when she told him about the urn popping open when she pushed on the cherubim, his brow burrowed in deep thought.

"Do you think—?" Paul began, then stopped abruptly when the diner's front door squeaked open, then quickly slammed shut. In the few seconds between the two sounds, the Curly and Carrot-top duo stumbled through the door. They were in the middle of another argument as they made their way to a table without waiting to be seated.

They took a place in the back, near where they'd been seated before, away from most of the customers. Carrot-top, however, was facing Kate. Directly in his line of vision, and hers, was the table with Collin, Renee, and Caroline.

Caroline obviously recognized the duo as they walked by. She whispered something to Collin, then inclined her head toward the back table. Kate wasn't within earshot of the conversation, but she imagined it had something to do with the GTO and Carrot-top and Curly, or "persons of interest," as Kate had called them the day she brought Caroline for ice cream.

Kate and Paul's meals arrived, with LuAnne carrying two platters on one arm and a basket of rolls in the opposite hand. Kate was pleased that Paul had taken her advice and ordered a grilled chicken salad and whole-wheat rolls. If he was keeping some awful news about his heart, or who knew what, from her, there was no time like the present to rev up that close watch on his cholesterol.

"Thank you, LuAnne," Paul said, standing to help her out. He reached for the rolls and placed the basket in the middle of the table while LuAnne placed the salads in front of them.

"*Lei è molto gentile*," she said.

Paul grinned. "And you are very kind as well."

"Now, how did you know what I just said?"

"Word's getting around," he said, sitting down again. "If you keep this up, half the town will learn conversational Italian."

Looking pleased, LuAnne adjusted the pencil over her ear and headed to the Curly and Carrot-top table. Kate noticed she had to wait briefly to get their order while the two seemed to be arguing about how much time they had and what they should get.

LuAnne was tapping her foot while she glanced around

the diner at the patrons waiting to be served. It was obvious her exasperation level had hit its limit. She stuck her pencil over her ear, tucked her pad in her apron pocket, and whirled to leave—all in one fluid motion.

She'd taken three steps when Carrot-top called after her: "Okay, okay. Just get us a couple of hamburgers, as fast as you can."

She put in their order, filled some coffee cups and water glasses, then hurried back to Kate and Paul.

"Somethin's comin' down, I just know it." She hitched one shoulder slightly toward Curly and Carrot-top.

"Have they said anything?" Kate asked.

She shook her head. "It's just the way they're actin', all nervous and jittery, like somethin' big is about to take place." She lowered her voice. "They've been in here a lot, but this is the worst. The one with the red hair's knocked over the salt-shaker three times."

Kate kept one eye on the back table while she and Paul ate their grilled chicken salads. Wanting to keep from being too obvious, Kate changed the subject. "Do you have your sermon ready for tomorrow morning?"

"Well," said Paul, "actually it's been a pretty eventful week, and I haven't had a lot of time for preparation. I'll need to spend some time tonight to firm up my outline. Then I can flesh things out a little more in the morning."

As they spoke, Kate noticed that Caroline kept turning her head to listen to what Curly and Carrot-top were saying, then whispering something to Collin and Renee. Kate's curiosity was making it nearly impossible to stay glued to her seat, but she didn't dare go over to ask what was going on.

She and Paul finished their meals, and when LuAnne brought their bill, Paul pulled out his wallet.

Kate reached for her handbag and was about to slide out of the booth, when Collin stood and walked over to Curly and Carrot-top's table. He spoke with them for a moment, then returned to his table and resumed his conversation with Renee and Caroline.

Immediately, the duo slammed some bills on the table and hightailed it to the door. They were both patting their pockets for their car keys as they stepped through the open doorway and let the door slam behind them.

Kate's heart thudded beneath her ribs as another dot connected. The boss's identity.

Everything pointed to Collin.

Paul and Kate turned to watch Renee. She was utterly aglow and seemed lost in deep conversation with Collin. He was holding her hand. Kate didn't want to let the charade go on any longer. She rose from her seat and walked over to Renee's table, smiling congenially at the three. Collin stood as she approached.

"I couldn't help but notice your, ah, interaction with the two who were sitting behind you," she said to Collin, keeping her tone even.

His piercing eyes were as cold as ever, his smile forced. "Ah yes, Mrs. Hanlon. You would wonder about them, wouldn't you?"

Kate glanced at Caroline, who said, "I told him you were keeping an eye on them as persons of interest."

Collin chuckled. "And if you must know, all I did was ask them to keep their voices down. Their language was—how shall I put this delicately?—unfit for the ears of the ladies who are with me."

"And they left because you asked them to?"

He laughed. "Of course not. I had nothing to do with how they scurried out of here, like rabbits heading to their warren." He paused. "One of them received a text message while I was talking to them. I would surmise that's why they so hurriedly vacated the premises."

I bet, Kate thought as she rejoined Paul at the entrance.

Chapter Twenty-Four

Kate woke to the sounds of distant thunder in the middle of the night. At first it rumbled across the valley from the mountains, then with each clap, it grew louder. Paul took Kate's hand as a streak of lightning lit the sky, followed immediately by a clap of thunder that seemed to break on top of their house. A downpour followed, and Kate snuggled close to Paul, trying to go back to sleep.

The rain continued through the wee hours of the morning, and finally at 4:51, Kate gave up on sleep, swung her feet over the side of the bed, and pulled on her robe. She padded to the kitchen and put on the coffee, chuckling to herself as she remembered the last time it rained.

It had been while Renee was in Italy and Kate and Paul were taking care of Kisses. When the thunderstorm hit, the little Chihuahua dove under the covers and curled in the crook of Paul's arm, quivering and whimpering in fear.

Paul softly sang to him, which seemed to be the only thing that would calm him down. Kate thought of the song, the sound of Paul's rich voice, and the lyrics that even then touched her heart: *"He is our peace, who has broken down every wall; He is our peace, He is our peace. Cast all your cares on Him, for He cares for you . . ."*

Another low rumble of thunder rolled across the valley as the storm moved east. The earlier downpour had turned into a steady rain about an hour before, and now in the glow of the ambient light from the kitchen, Kate could see only a misty rain falling on the maple-tree leaves and the yard beyond.

She walked into the living room, sat down in her rocker, and reached for her Bible. For a few minutes she held it on her lap without opening it. She was the one who needed peace right now.

"Cast all your cares on Him . . ."

She thought about the financial trouble she and Paul were in and wondered how and when he would finally tell her. Maybe he thought that because of her worries over Mia, it would be better to wait until they knew for certain what her treatment would be.

"For He cares for you . . ."

She knew this to be true in her heart, but sometimes, like right now, she wanted to be the one tucked in God's great arms, listening to his voice singing to her. *"Cast all your cares on me . . . for I care for you . . . I am your peace, Kate. I am your peace."*

She thought about the image of Paul cuddling the tiny Chihuahua, and of God cuddling her, for a moment, and smiled. If Paul knew how much she was fretting over all this, would he still ask her to trust him? Would he still keep silent?

She went into the kitchen, poured her coffee, and glanced

at the counter where Paul had left the previous day's unopened mail.

The stack, with its usual jumble of ads and flyers, had slid off to one side of the telephone. It was in need of sorting, and in anticipation of their busy Sunday, she reached for the entire stack. Bending over the counter, she sorted out the real mail, then tossed the junk mail into the trash under the sink.

She idly glanced at the unopened envelopes, then frowned as she picked up an envelope with the Mid-Cumberland Bank's return address. Thinking it might be their latest statement, she opened it. It was a confirmation of a new safety-deposit box, thanking Paul for his business. She looked at the envelope again and blinked. The new account was in Paul's name only.

THE RAIN DIDN'T DAMPEN the spirits of the parishioners that morning. As Kate walked down the aisle toward her usual pew, she heard someone call her name.

It was Renee, with Collin at her side.

Renee waggled her fingers. She was dressed in pale pink, from coiffed tip to high-heeled toe, and wore a cape that definitely gave her a European flair. Her French manicure was freshly done, and the usual scent of Youth-Dew floated down the aisle with her.

Collin smiled at those he knew from the tour. Millie Lovelace was the first to come up to him, gushing about how glad she was to see him at Faith Briar, reminding him that she was the church secretary. The Jenners stepped up next. He bowed and kissed Livvy's fingers and then shook Danny's hand.

Then his gaze locked onto Kate's, and though he smiled in greeting, the smile stopped well below his piercing eyes. He bent to kiss her fingers, and when he stood upright again, it was clear that his unblinking, cold expression held a warning even more severe than before.

Kate shivered, but gave him a weak smile. "I'm glad you could join us."

"We'll sit with you," Renee announced and pushed her way into the pew. Kate stood back while the couple got settled, then she slid in beside Renee.

Paul stepped up onto the platform, followed by Sam Gorman, who seated himself at the organ and began to play "To God Be the Glory."

A few minutes later, the congregation stood and joined in, lifting their voices in song. As the last notes faded and while the congregation remained standing, Paul moved to the pulpit to read the opening Scripture, Psalm 95:1–2: "Oh come, let us sing to the Lord! Let us shout joyfully to the Rock of our salvation. Let us come before His presence with thanksgiving . . ."

When Paul finished, he nodded to Sam, and the choir members took their places in front of the platform near the organ. Kate stepped into the back row next to Renee.

While Sam played the introduction, Renee held her hymnal over her mouth and whispered to Kate, "There's somebody moving around in the foyer. I can see their shadows moving across the strip where the double doors come together."

Kate squinted toward the doors, but she couldn't see what Renee was talking about. Renee was standing in the center of the choir in a direct lineup with the double doors.

If she had moved a few inches one way or the other, she wouldn't have noticed anything unusual.

Kate glanced at Paul, who was sitting to one side of the pulpit, slightly behind her. But he was looking down as if in prayer. After a moment of silence, he stood and led the congregation in the opening prayer.

As the worshippers echoed a loud "Amen," the organ introduction swelled. Then Sam gave the choir a nod, and they began to sing, *"I come to the garden alone, while the dew is still on the roses . . ."*

Renee was still distracted. Staring at the double doors instead of at Samuel or the hymnal, she sang verse two while everyone else was singing verse one. But Kate didn't think anyone else noticed.

"There," she whispered to Kate during the organ's bridge between verses. "I see them again."

Kate thought of the Diner Duo, and her heart caught. Would they have the audacity to rob the church during Sunday services?

"He speaks, and the sound of His voice is so sweet the birds hush their singing . . . ," the rest of the choir sang, then Sam gestured to the congregation to stand again and join the choir on the chorus. *"And He walks with me, and He talks with me, and He tells me I am His own . . ."*

Just then, the sanctuary doors opened.

Kate stopped singing midnote and just stared.

Toddling down the center aisle, holding Mommy's hand on one side and Daddy's on the other, was Mia Elizabeth. She wore a happy smile, and when she saw Kate, she let go of Melissa's hand and frantically waved to her grandmother.

Kate couldn't help herself. She quickly slipped from her place in the choir into the aisle and scooped Mia into her arms, squeezing her tight. Mia, looking over Kate's shoulder, giggled when she saw Paul and called out "Gampa, Gampa."

Sam finished leading a rather raggedy *"And the joy we share as we tarry there, none other has ever known,"* then all the choir members, with the exception of Kate, filed back to their seats. Paul came down from the platform to stand beside Kate at the front of the sanctuary, and Mia reached out to be taken into her grandfather's arms.

"We follow where the Spirit leads here at Faith Briar," Paul said, "and that means things don't always go as planned. I know you all have been holding Mia and her mom and dad—and her grandparents—in prayer over the past couple of weeks. So I'd like to take a brief break in our normal routine and ask Melissa and John to tell everyone the latest medical news about Mia."

Melissa's eyes were glistening with tears as she came up to stand by her mother, but Kate knew her daughter well: they were tears of joy.

"God is so good," John said, his voice breaking.

Melissa jumped in, taking his hand. "He answered the prayers of our heart."

PAUL HAD PUT A POT of chili on before church, and it was steaming hot and waiting for them when they arrived home. Kate poured the corn bread batter into a pan, then slipped it into the oven. She and Melissa worked together to chop some onions and grate a block of cheddar cheese while the corn bread baked.

Paul and Kate set the table, insisting that Melissa and John relax for a few minutes and telephone Melissa's siblings—Andrew and Rachel in Philadelphia, and Rebecca in New York—with their good news. The phone was passed around, and after her turn, Kate sat back, enjoying the familiar banter and laughter and wishing her brood was gathered there in person.

The timer chimed and the fragrance of corn bread filled the room as Kate pulled the pan from the oven. John's eyes lit up when he lifted the lid on the pot of chili, and Melissa sighed when she saw two lemon-meringue pies come out of the fridge.

When they had taken their places at the table, they held hands as Paul lifted a prayer of thanksgiving heavenward.

The first sound following the prayer came from Mia. She sat in her high chair waving her spoon over her applesauce and stringing sounds together that sounded like blue pancakes. Her cheeks were rosy again, and her eyes sparkled with life.

After dinner, the family lingered around the table over second helpings of Kate's pies, still rejoicing over the good news and talking about the treatments the doctors recommended, and the best news of all: The doctors fully expected her heart to heal itself as she grew older. They would monitor her carefully, of course, but they expected her to fully enjoy a healthy childhood.

Mia took a drink of milk from her sippy cup and buzzed her lips, giggled, and tried it again. She pounded the spoon on the high-chair tray, then decided to give her stuffed bunny rabbit a drink of her milk.

John turned the conversation to Kate, asking about the mysterious urn. She caught them up with the latest. Paul filled in details about meeting Collin at Renee's tea, and Kate told them about running into him at church the previous day, holding the urn and climbing the stairs from the basement.

"It's the strangest thing," she said. "After he left, I opened the urn, which was a surprise because we hadn't been able to open it before. It had obviously been tampered with, so I searched the basement to see if anything unusual turned up."

"Something tells me it did," Melissa said, smiling at her mother.

"Just a strange little square battery, and I'm not even sure it was his. I found it in one of the classrooms—in the trash."

"A square battery?" John frowned. "You mean like a nine-volt?"

Kate shook her head. "More the size of a postage stamp."

She got up and headed to the bedroom, where she'd left her handbag. A moment later she returned, unwrapped the tissue, and handed it to John.

He laid it on his palm, turned it over, and then looked up at Kate. "This isn't a battery," he said. "It's a computer chip." He held it to the light. "And it appears to be a dud."

"A dud?"

"As in it was on the receiving end of a power surge or something else that might have caused it to malfunction. You can see where the tiny contacts melted together." He held it out for Kate to see.

"That's why the chip was thrown away," Kate said, her mind in a whirl. "It needed to be replaced."

Chapter Twenty-Five

Computer chip?

Kate couldn't get the little defunct chip out of her mind. The kids had gone to bed at eight thirty in anticipation of their trip home the following day, and Paul said he also needed to turn in early. He had a morning business appointment in Pine Ridge. They were exhausted from all they had been through, and he'd promised to help them settle in. Again, there was no invitation for Kate to join him.

As soon as the house was quiet, Kate sat at the kitchen table. Her heart ached that once again Paul was going off to another appointment, leaving her in the dark about their finances. Why wouldn't he invite her to join him? How she longed to know what was going on. How she wanted to share the heavy burden with the husband she loved so much, but he had chosen to carry it alone.

She bowed her head and sat in silence for several moments. *Lord, you know how much I love Paul, and how willing I am to help in any way I can. For whatever reason, he has chosen to leave me out of the picture. Please give me the patience to abide by his wishes. And keep me from feeling resentment toward him.*

After she opened her eyes, she remembered the tiny chip in her hand, and a million scenarios tried themselves on for size in her brain. She glanced at the clock. It wasn't too late for what she needed to do.

She tiptoed into the bedroom to retrieve her handbag, keys—to the car and to the church—and a light sweater. Then she slipped back toward the entry door leading to the garage.

Three minutes later, she backed out onto the street and turned the Honda toward Mountain Laurel, where she turned left and then left again into the church parking lot.

A security light illumined the front of the church, and the spotlight in the steeple gave the beloved Faith Briar bell a luminous glow. It always brought her comfort to see that bell and its reminder of how God, after the church burned, truly gave the little congregation beauty for ashes and the oil of joy for mourning.

She hurried to the entrance and unlocked the door, being careful to lock it behind her after she stepped inside. The Diner Duo was still part of the puzzle, and though she didn't know exactly how they fit into the bigger picture, she didn't want to be taken by surprise if they showed up.

She turned on the light to the foyer and headed to the glass case, though the framed Saint Francis quote that Renee had borrowed and hung beside the case caught her attention for a moment. Maybe it was the way the overhead light shone on the glass, but something made her focus on the words "It is in giving that we receive . . . ," and she paused, thinking of

Paul and the burden he had been carrying by himself. She lifted a quick prayer for him, then, as she stood in front of the print, she had a thought.

What if she could somehow help out financially? Though she had put them aside briefly to work on her new stained-glass votive design, she had been working on two new Tiffany-style lamps over the past few months, planning to enter them in the county fair. Maybe she could offer them for sale at the same time—plus take orders for more, if others were interested. She wouldn't be able to make up the thousands they obviously owed, but it would be a start. This would be a gift to Paul to ease whatever it was that burdened him, a gift of love.

She smiled to herself as she located the key in Millie's office, then opened the glass case, where the urn glowed beneath the spotlight.

Her heart beat in anticipation as she took the urn into her hands. She knelt and placed it on the floor, pressed the cherubim's tiny feet, and the urn snapped open.

At first glance, the inside space was empty. But something at the back of her mind suspected there might be a secret cavity—a space where the computer chip had been hidden.

Gingerly she moved her fingers around the space where the sides met the bottom, turning the urn toward the light so she could peer inside. Suddenly she saw it. A tiny aperture in one corner. Barely visible, the opening couldn't have been much wider than a toothpick. Did it lead to some kind of false bottom?

She remembered John's "smart phone," and the little stylus

that he often used with it. Something like that would have been perfect for her purposes, but John and his phone weren't there.

What about a safety pin? She didn't need it often, but she kept a sewing kit the size of a matchbook in her handbag. She reached for it, rummaged around inside, then pulled out the kit.

A moment later, fingers shaking, she pressed the opened pin into the tiny hole.

Nothing happened. She tried once more. Still nothing.

She sat back in disappointment. When she saw that little aperture, she had been sure that the urn had a false bottom.

She looked at the pin and bit her lower lip. She needed something a little larger. Something like . . . a coin! Again, she rummaged around in her handbag, found her coin purse, and grabbed a penny.

Holding the coin between her thumb and index finger, she then pressed its edge into the aperture.

As if by magic, whatever was holding the false bottom in place released.

Kate sat back with a satisfied smile. *A penny urned* . . . and suppressed a nervous giggle.

Then bad pun forgotten, her eyes widened in surprise.

Chapter Twenty-Six

Kate stared at the device inside the urn. At first, with her heart thudding beneath her ribs, she thought it might be a bomb. She blinked at it a few minutes, holding the urn utterly still, and considered the headlines in the *Chronicle* that week: Minister's Wife Blown to Bits by Urn Bomb.

Her nervousness was affecting her sense of humor. First the bad pun, now the "explosive" headline. She stifled a groan, drew in a deep breath, then peered more intently at the device.

Whatever it was had been in need of a new computer chip. And Collin had taken it downstairs and into a Sunday-school classroom, seemingly so he could avoid being discovered should someone come into the church unexpectedly.

She touched the small device, checking to see whether it would budge. It was somewhat bigger than a cell phone, perhaps the size of a GPS.

A GPS? She almost gasped. She knew that kind of techie item could help people find their way through traffic or let them know where they were on any given back road.

But why would such a device be installed in an urn that might—or might not—be an ancient artifact?

A half second later, the obvious answer hit her brain: A museum could have installed it as a tracking device—if the piece was indeed the original.

What, then, had Collin done with it? Could he have replaced the museum's chip with one of his own? If so, why?

Her brain was beginning to hurt from all the possibilities.

She closed the compartment in the urn, turning the cherubim to their original positions.

Then she placed the urn back in the case and locked it. After returning the key to Millie's desk, she headed to the door, stopped, and glanced back at the glowing urn once more.

With more questions whirling through her mind than before, she turned out the light and stepped outside into the dark parking lot.

PAUL LEFT BEFORE SUNUP for his appointment in Pine Ridge. While he was gone, the kids packed the car to leave while Kate read picture books to Mia.

When Paul returned, they said their good-byes and cleared out of the house so quickly, Kate didn't have a chance to tell anyone her astonishing discovery the night before.

As soon as the breakfast dishes were washed and put away, she called Livvy. "I need to run something by you."

"I have a meeting at noon, but how about coffee this morning? If you'd like, we can get together in one of the conference rooms upstairs."

Kate laughed with her. "How about tenish?"

"I'll see you then . . ." Livvy hesitated. "Kate, do I detect a note of sleuthing success in your voice?"

Kate laughed. "Just a few more pieces of the puzzle fitting together. But it's such a bizarre theory, I need to run it by my sleuthing partner."

"I figured you'd be spending time with Paul today."

"He left early this morning, first for business in Pine Ridge, then to follow the kids to Atlanta. He's planning to spend the night."

Surprisingly, Livvy didn't ask any questions or sound the least bit sympathetic about Paul's secrecy. She just said she would see Kate at ten and disconnected the call.

Kate sat at the kitchen table, staring at the receiver. Again, she sensed her best friend knew something that she didn't.

More puzzled than ever, she replaced the phone and headed to her studio.

She glanced at the votive designs she'd been working on, and then filed them away. Saint Francis would have his day later. It was time to concentrate on the Tiffany table lamps. She lifted one onto her worktable, admiring the colors and design. Both lamps still lacked the electrical hookups and needed to be mounted to their bases, but their stained-glass shades were complete.

In a twist of irony, she had planned them as gifts for Paul after the county fair—one for his office at church, and one for his home study. The colors were his favorites and the designs, two he had long admired.

She jotted down some ideas for the fair exhibit, a pricing list, and the approximate time the buyer could expect her to take to complete the project. She quickly did the math, figuring in her time and materials and the cost of the oil-rubbed bronze bases and electrical work, then factored in the number she would have to sell to help make up the money they owed. She sat back and blinked.

It was almost overwhelming, but she would do anything to help the man she loved. They were in this together, and when he decided the time was right, she would present the gift of her time and talents to him.

AT A FEW MINUTES BEFORE TEN, Kate parked in front of the library. When she reached the conference room on the second floor, Livvy had already poured their coffee and was seated at one end of the rectangular table.

She met Kate with a smile. "I can see by the gleam in your eye that you're onto something."

Kate sat down next to her friend and took a sip of coffee. "I am. At least I think I am, but some of this is so far-fetched . . ." She laughed. "Besides Paul, you're the best sounding board I know."

"I'll take that as a compliment," Livvy said with a wink. "Tell me what you've found out."

Kate sat back in her chair. "Let me see if I can pull all this together in my own mind." She paused for a moment, collecting her wild whirl of thoughts. "The duo we both observed in the diner—"

"Curly and Carrot-top?" Livvy giggled.

Kate grinned. "Don't get me started."

"You've seen them since that day they locked themselves out of the car?"

"Twice at the diner, once at Emma's, and a fleeting glance as they left the diner when I was driving by. To me, it seems they're waiting for their boss to give them some signal."

"And you think it has to do with stealing the urn?"

Kate nodded. "I'm almost certain of it."

"Which means the urn isn't a copy, and Collin simply used Renee to get it into the US."

"He definitely used her for transporting it internationally—just as he used you to write the article about it and plant the photos in the paper."

Livvy narrowed her eyes in thought. "Why would he do that?"

Kate sipped her coffee thoughtfully. "Think about his motives. He apparently wanted publicity, as much as possible. He must have targeted this area of Tennessee for a purpose. After all, he targeted the tour bus that had two large magnetic signs announcing "Tennesseans Tour Tuscany." But why Tennessee?" she wondered out loud. "Do you suppose there's some connection between Collin and Dr. Hosea?"

Livvy leaned back and crossed her arms. "Wow. That would be something. Okay, I follow you so far. What else?"

"We don't know who the boss is that Curly and Carrot-top are waiting for . . ."

"It could even be someone here in Copper Mill since we seem to be the center of this intrigue with the urn."

Kate nodded. "True." She paused and drew in a deep breath. "Then there's the urn itself. I've discovered how to open it."

Livvy leaned forward, obviously impressed. "You did? How in the world did you figure it out?"

Kate explained, then told Livvy about running into Collin Saturday morning at the church.

"He took the urn downstairs. I met him just as he was coming back up. Then he returned the urn to the glass case and left, though not without giving me another stern warning."

"Just like the last one . . . to stay away?"

"The same." Kate tucked a strand of hair behind one ear. "I think something's about to go down. The signs are all there."

"Another heist?"

Kate nodded. "Only this one from our very own Faith Briar." She paused for a moment, gathering her thoughts before going on. "There was a false bottom in the urn, and I opened it with a penny."

Livvy laughed. "As in 'a penny ur—'"

Kate grinned. "Exactly." She sipped her coffee, then put the cup down and leaned her elbows on the table. "Livvy, there was this device inside, something that appeared to be a GPS."

"Why isn't the urn being heavily guarded? I mean, if there's any chance it might be stolen, shouldn't the sheriff or his deputy be in on this?"

"I agree, and I plan to call the sheriff and let him know what I've discovered. Skip was concerned about the man he saw running from the church, though nothing ever came of it."

"The sheriff or Skip will probably plan a few more drive-bys, don't you think?" Livvy took a sip of her coffee.

"I certainly don't have the evidence it would take for Skip to do a stakeout." She bit her lower lip in thought. "But I can't let this go. I want to catch these guys red-handed."

She picked up her coffee cup and scooted back her chair. Livvy stood with her. "So you're going to do this by yourself, aren't you? I can see it now, the minister's wife camping out in the sanctuary, waiting for some international thieves to arrive." She laughed.

"Actually, that's exactly what I was thinking," Kate said. "How else can I catch them red-handed?"

"From everything you've told me, this is getting more and more dangerous. You can't go alone."

Kate raised an eyebrow. "If you're hinting about going with me, I can't let you. I don't want to put you in danger."

Livvy grinned, her eyes sparkling. "Are you kidding? I wouldn't miss this for the world."

Kate took a last sip of coffee. "Okay Liv. But we're both going to have to be extra watchful." Kate paused, brushing her fingers through the crown of her hair. "In my way of thinking, tonight's the night for the hit. Mondays are notoriously slow days at the church. On most Mondays, there's hardly a sign of life in the church or the parking lot."

"I figure the thieves most likely won't attempt a break-in in broad daylight." She sat back and folded her arms with a smile. "If they're planning to pick the perfect time for a church robbery, it will be a Monday night."

"Are you going to tell that to the sheriff?"

"Of course. And I hope he listens. But either way, I plan to be there."

"Okay," Livvy said, picking up their Styrofoam coffee cups and dumping them in the trash. "What time?"

Kate gave her a big grin. "Somehow I knew you'd ask. As soon as you get off work. I'll meet you there. I'm figuring it may be an all-night vigil."

They left the conference room and headed to the computer

bank where Kate placed her handbag next to one of the computers. Before sitting down, she studied her friend thoughtfully. "You know what it all comes down to?"

Livvy shook her head.

"It's not the urn itself that counts—whether it's real or just a good copy. It's not even whether it's stolen from Faith Briar." She paused. "What really counts is the harm Collin's deceit will cause Renee, and it breaks my heart."

"We're doing this for Renee," Livvy said. "And Collin Wellington better come up with some pretty solid answers, or he'll have all of Copper Mill to deal with."

Kate smiled. "I couldn't have said it better myself."

Livvy left to return to her office downstairs, and Kate sat down and turned on the computer. She typed in her password and clicked on the mail logo. There were the usual ads, plus a few from friends, then at the very bottom, an e-mail from Dr. Hosea. On the subject line, it read, *New Information About the Urn. Important!*

She clicked it open and began to read,

Dear Kate,

I thought you might be interested in the attached article that just came across my desk.

Sincerely,
Reg

She clicked on the article header, which read, "Replicas of Ancient Artifacts Found to Contain Trace Amounts of Anthrax."

Kate's heart skipped a beat. Could she have overlooked that powdery substance in her excitement? She had touched the urn's interior, looking for a way to open the false bottom. Surely she would have noticed a white powder on her fingers.

There had been nothing.

She clicked on Google and typed "GPS" into the search window. Instantly, hundreds of hits came up, mostly electronic stores where one could purchase them.

She needed to narrow her search. She typed in "GPS tracking device," then sat back, crossing her arms as articles came up that confirmed her suspicions.

Chapter Twenty-Seven

Dusk was falling as Kate parked the Honda a short distance from the church. No other cars were on the road, and the parking lot had been empty when she drove by. It was eerily quiet, and getting darker by the minute, as a bank of clouds moved over Copper Mill, obscuring the setting sun.

Thunderheads had been building all afternoon; now she heard the rumble of distant thunder. She shivered and hoped Livvy would hurry.

Fifteen minutes passed. Then ten more. It wasn't like Livvy to be late. Kate was getting worried.

Three minutes later, she checked the rearview mirror. Headlights winked back at her from the distance, coming from Smoky Mountain Road—not a route that Livvy would take from the library—then turning right onto Mountain Laurel.

Kate slid down in the seat and waited until the vehicle passed. She could think of at least a half-dozen other Hondas of similar make in Copper Mill. She hoped that fact alone would protect her from looking like she was on some sort of stakeout. She eased up slightly, her eyes just above the bottom of the window.

A dark car pulled off the road into the same undergrowth and wooded ivy where Collin had parked on Saturday. She couldn't see the make of the car from where she was parked.

Kate had hoped Skip would drive by in the black-and-white SUV—as he'd said he would. But so far she hadn't seen him. As the minutes ticked by, she was becoming even more worried about Livvy.

Finally, Kate couldn't wait any longer. She slipped out of the Honda, barely letting the door click shut behind her, and moved silently toward the vehicle. She heard the rustle of footsteps ahead of her in the dark.

She felt the first dollop of rain. Then another. She sighed as the rain steadily increased and the wind kicked up.

Someone was obviously heading to the back door of the church, a little-used entrance that opened into a small room—used mostly by Paul and Sam for prayer before services—off the raised platform at the front of the sanctuary. A third door led directly into the sanctuary.

Kate fell back into the brush, hiding as the shadowy male figure fiddled with the lock for a moment, then opened the door. He glanced around, then let himself inside.

The rain was falling faster now, and Kate shivered. She looked back toward the car, hoping to see that Livvy had pulled up behind her and parked.

Or that Skip was cruising by slowly, using his spotlight and peering toward the church.

Her heart fell.

She would be soaking wet if she stayed outside much longer to wait for either of them. Closing her eyes and whispering a small prayer, she waited until she thought whoever it was had moved into the sanctuary, and perhaps to the foyer.

Kate unlocked the door and pushed it open a few inches. She listened quietly for several seconds, and then, hearing nothing, pulled her penlight out of her pocket and flicked the beam around the room.

Empty.

Mustering her courage, she moved inside, leaving the door open a crack for Livvy, should she follow. Then holding her breath, Kate stood by the door leading to the sanctuary and listened for signs of life—footsteps, rustles of movement, anything that would tell her Collin was nearby.

An eerie silence reigned.

She pressed against the door, opening it incrementally until she could look through. The sanctuary was utterly dark.

She slipped through the doorway and, feeling her way along the first pew, found the aisle. She moved silently and slowly, almost afraid to breathe.

Halfway to the foyer's double doors, Kate heard voices in the foyer. She quickly slipped into a pew and ducked down to the floor. If someone pushed through the doors, she didn't want to be standing in their way.

She recognized the voices in the foyer. The backwoods' drawls of Curly and Carrot-top. And one other voice sounded familiar, but she couldn't quite place it.

Then she heard a fourth voice. There was no mistaking whose it was. And the sound of it caused Kate's blood to freeze in her veins.

It was Livvy. And she sounded scared, or hurt. Or both. Pounding and crying and shouting for help.

Chapter Twenty-Eight

At almost the same time that Livvy screamed, a jagged flash of lightning split open the sky through the side window.

Kate gasped and jerked back, tripping over the pew in her hurry to get away.

There on the floor beside where she had been squatting lay a body. And in that split second of light, there was no mistaking the body's identity. Or the missing puzzle pieces that rushed into her head . . . and connected.

Collin Wellington. His head bloodied. His face as pale as the alabaster urn.

In a heartbeat, Kate was beside him, searching for a pulse.

Collin moaned as Kate lifted his wrist. His pulse was faint and irregular, but he was alive.

She sat there for a moment, trying to decide what to do. The muffled sounds of scurrying about in the foyer carried into the sanctuary. She hadn't heard Livvy's voice again, which terrified her even more. It also made her more determined to break through the foyer doors and take the thieves by surprise.

A clap of thunder rolled nearby, shaking the little church. Kate's heart thundered with it.

It occurred to her that Collin probably had a weapon. She didn't know much about such things, but it might at least help her scare off the thieves and save Livvy.

She felt Collin's ankle, thinking that was where he might carry a concealed weapon. There was nothing there.

The small of his back was another she'd heard about, but with the shape he was in, she couldn't roll him over. She patted his torso, hoping above all hope that he might have a holstered weapon hidden there.

He surprised her when he spoke. "Do you know who . . . I am?" he whispered.

She rocked back on her heels, staring at him. It took her a minute to gather the thoughts that had come flying into her head the moment she saw him. "My guess is Scotland Yard or maybe MI6," she said.

He tried to sit up but groaned and fell back again. "How long . . . have you known?"

"I didn't put it all together until just now. But my first clue was the computer chip, then I found the tracking device. Things began to come together; this is a sting operation. I just didn't know you were the head of it, at least until I saw what the thugs did to you."

There was admiration in his voice. "I . . . tried to warn . . . you."

"You're not off the hook," Kate whispered. "You used my friend for your own purposes—"

He started to protest but groaned again.

In the foyer, there was more scrambling, pounding, scraping, and above it all, Livvy shouting for help.

Kate had to do something. And fast.

Collin tried to get up but fell back again. "My other foot," he whispered. "That's where it is."

"I don't know the first thing about guns," Kate said, quickly retrieving it.

"Just take . . . the safety . . . off. Please. You may need it."

"I'll leave it as it is," she said, her heart thumping wildly. "It's the element of surprise I'm counting on." *And prayer*. Big-time prayer.

She pulled out her cell phone and tossed it to Collin. "Call the sheriff," she said. "He's on auto-dial."

She stood up and, putting her shoulders back, headed to the double doors. Holding the gun straight out in front of her with both hands the way she'd seen it done on TV, she swept through the doorway.

"Hold it right there!" she shouted with every bit of sternness she could muster. "The first one to move will be sorry."

She hoped no one noticed her knees quaking.

Three men stared at her. Curly gaped. Carrot-top sneered. And Dr. Reg Hosea, who was holding the urn, stared at the gun. It occurred to her that one of the smarter fellows might be able to tell that the safety was still on.

"What about the anthrax?" she said to him. Then she added, "Never mind. I already know it was a hoax, and not a very original one at that. It was that last e-mail, trying to scare me off, that cinched it for me."

"Cinched what?" Curly wanted to know.

"That Dr. Hosea wasn't who he'd led me to believe."

"How'd you know?" This from Reg himself.

"You didn't know about the Etruscan language, even after I asked you what the symbols meant. The information you fed me about Francis and Clare was vague and uncertain. You also didn't know about the secret locking device on the urn."

"It opens?" Curly scowled at the urn, still in Dr. Hosea's hands. "Why?"

"To hold ashes, you dolt," Carrot-top said.

Curly's expression turned to horror. "You mean that thing could have ashes—human remains—inside?" He visibly shuddered.

Dr. Hosea started to move toward Kate, but she held the pistol on him. "Something tells me a minister's wife wouldn't know the first thing about shooting a gun," he said with a sneer.

"Don't count on that," Livvy shouted from behind Millie Lovelace's office. There was a chair propped under the handle, locking her in. "We go skeet shooting together. Once a week. She was champion in her age group. Three times. You better do what she says."

Kate's mouth dropped open. She'd never heard her friend lie before. She supposed it was for a good cause, but knowing Livvy, she'd be on her knees pleading for forgiveness later.

"Right now, I say let my friend out from behind the door." She was looking at Curly, who was still pale from the news about the ashes.

"Go!" she said.

"Hurry!" Livvy said and pounded the door again for emphasis. "You have no idea how dangerous this woman can be."

Just as he started for the office door, Carrot-top lunged for Kate. She stumbled backward at the exact moment Collin burst through the foyer doors, looking pale and shaken, his forehead bloodied, but walking, and holding a revolver (four times the size of the one in Kate's hands).

"I wouldn't do that if I were you," he said to Carrot-top and motioned him back.

"And you," he said to Curly, waving the gun at him, "do as the lady said."

Curly pulled the chair out from under the knob, and Livvy, who'd obviously been pushing hard against the opposite side of the door, spilled into the foyer.

Dr. Hosea stepped forward menacingly, staring at Collin. When he spoke, his voice came out in a growl. "Drop the gun or say good-bye to the urn." He held it out, shifting it slightly so that it wobbled precariously on his fingertips. "I don't have to tell you that its value is beyond price or what the world will lose should I drop it."

Collin didn't budge. The revolver was trained on Hosea.

"Maybe you didn't hear me," Dr. Hosea growled again. "I drop it, and no one will ever lay eyes on this treasure again. Not the Exeter, not you, not Scotland Yard. No one."

For a moment, the only sound in the room was Curly's nervous breathing.

Collin glanced at Kate just long enough for her to see the glint of mischief in his eyes. "What do you think? Shall we let him do it?"

The others in the room gasped.

Kate couldn't help smiling. "I'd say go for it," she said to Dr. Hosea.

Dr. Reginald Hosea set his lips in a thin angry line, then, almost as if in slow motion, he released the urn from his fingertips.

It crashed to the floor, shattering in what Kate thought was surely a million pieces.

Chapter Twenty-Nine

Oh no! Were there ashes in it?" Curly patted his pockets for his keys and backed toward the exit to the parking lot.

"No, you imbecile," Carrot-top said, "no ashes, but look at that."

"What?" Curly wanted to know.

"The thing that looks like a cell phone."

"That was inside where the ashes were supposed to be?" Curly stepped toward the shattered urn and stooped to have a look. "Well, I'll be a monkey's uncle."

Dr. Hosea seemed oblivious to everything but the shattered urn . . . until Carrot-top dropped the electronic device in the ersatz archaeologist's palm.

He looked up at Collin. "So it wasn't the original after all," he said. "This was placed inside to track the fake?"

"Until it needed a new computer chip, we knew its location within a few feet one direction or the other." Collin shot Kate a smile. "I almost pulled off the chip-switch without a glitch, but this sleuth caught me red-handed." He looked back to Dr. Hosea. "The original has been with Scotland Yard for weeks."

"How did you get it?"

"It seems that after the Oxford heist, your dynamic duo here headed straight for Florence in a stolen Brink's truck and some sort of a rendezvous—presumably with the kingpin of the operation."

Hosea kept his lips in a straight line and didn't comment.

Collin went on. "The stolen Brink's vehicle wasn't exactly invisible, so Interpol had an eye on it, at least until it disappeared in the Chunnel. From what we've pieced together, they stopped at a café just outside Florence and left the vehicle unlocked with the stolen urn in back. While they were eating, the Brink's truck was stolen right out from under their noses, urn and all. The vehicle was later abandoned. When the police found it, they contacted Interpol, and they in turn contacted Scotland Yard."

Hosea looked confused. "Why all this elaborate scheming then? You got your valuable artifact, wasn't that enough?"

Collin smiled. "No, we wanted you, the long-suspected crooked collector of ancient, and usually priceless, artifacts."

Outside, a stream of vehicles with sirens and flashing lights flooded into the parking lot. Seconds later the doors burst open, and Sheriff Alan Roberts and his deputy, Skip Spencer, entered, guns drawn.

"We've got it under control," Collin said. "Thank you for getting here so fast."

Kate glanced at Livvy, who gave her a thumbs-up, her smile wide.

"SKEET-SHOOTING CHAMPION?" Kate said to Livvy as she dodged a puddle near where Livvy's car was parked.

Livvy had just finished telling her how she was apprehended by Curly and Carrot-top when they recognized her from the diner. She had just pulled into the parking lot, looking for Kate, when Curly jumped in front of her car, then acted as if she'd hit him. When she stopped to investigate, Carrot-top grabbed her from behind and dragged her into the church, then jammed her into Millie Lovelace's office.

She grinned at Kate. "I couldn't think of anything believable for a minister's wife to shoot. Skeet shooting is a sport that doesn't kill anything, plus . . . it was the first thing that came to my mind."

They stopped next to Livvy's car.

"So what do you think about Renee's Collin now?" Livvy said as she opened the driver's side door.

"He may be a hero as far as Scotland Yard is concerned, but in my book, he hasn't redeemed himself. He used Renee, and that's not right." Kate thought of all that had happened to Renee in her past. Her losses. Her heartaches. She blinked back fresh tears. "And now someone has to tell her."

"He's walking toward us right now," Livvy said. "Actually, make that limping toward us."

Kate turned. Collin lifted his hand in greeting, then stopped a dozen yards away as if too weary to take another step. "I'm about to be transported to the hospital," he said. "But I'm wondering if I might have a word with you first, Mrs. Hanlon."

Kate said good-bye to Livvy, then walked over to Collin.

"Whatever it is can wait. You do need to get someone to look at that wound immediately."

"I've had worse," he said. "But what I have to tell you is far more important."

Kate helped him walk back toward the waiting EMT van. He leaned against her slightly as they walked.

"It's about Renee," he said. "I know you think I used her for this sting operation. And I suppose that was my intent at the beginning." He paused, and in the ambient light of the law-enforcement vehicles, Kate caught the glisten of tears in his eyes.

"But after we spent time together, I found I was falling in love." He laughed lightly. "Imagine such a thing at my age. And the wonder of it all was that this beautiful, talented, delightful woman said she was falling in love with me." He wiped his eyes.

"I know you're thinking the worst of me, and I suppose even the fact that I planned the way we met—"

"Because she was from Tennessee, and you were trying to flush out Dr. Reginald Hosea," Kate filled in.

"Exactly. I had been watching for such an opportunity when I bumped into Renee during the sudden cloudburst in Rome."

They had almost reached the van. Collin turned his head toward Kate. "Do you know what she said to me when I covered her with my rain cape?"

Kate shook her head.

"She said, 'Where have you been all my life? I've been waiting for you.' And when she smiled at me, I felt the same way."

The paramedics helped him onto a gurney and started to push it into the back of the van. Collin reached for Kate's hand.

"I want to marry her, if she'll do me the honor." He smiled and squeezed Kate's hand weakly. "And if she'll agree to make her home with me in Oxford with her mother . . . and even that little mouse of a dog."

The paramedics pushed the gurney the remaining distance into the van, slammed the doors, and drove off.

Kate stood where she was, stunned. Renee and Caroline and Kisses moving to England?

Copper Mill wouldn't be the same without them.

Chapter Thirty

Wednesday morning, Renee called Kate and invited herself over for a cup of tea.

Kate had planned to spend the day working on a new Tiffany lamp for the county fair, to give potential buyers the choice of another pattern. But as soon as she heard the catch in Renee's voice, she readily agreed.

Fifteen minutes later, Renee appeared at the parsonage door. She had a large, fashionable tote bag in one hand, and the new Italian leather leash in the other, with Kisses, of course, attached to the opposite end.

She bustled in as usual without waiting to be invited and headed immediately for the kitchen. "You've had a rough few days, so just sit down and rest your weary bones while I make us some tea."

Renee busied herself around Kate's small kitchen while Kate sat down at the table to watch. Snoring sounds drifted in from the sofa in the living room where Kisses had curled up for a nap.

"How is Collin?" Kate asked.

Renee didn't answer right away. She pulled out a bottle of designer water from her tote, then poured it into the teakettle.

"He's resting well. The doctor says he'll be released from the hospital tomorrow." She poured hot tap water into the teapot that had once belonged to Kate's grandmother and set it aside to warm.

They chatted for a few minutes about Collin's heroism on Monday night, his work with Scotland Yard, and the deception over the urn, which seemed not to bother Renee in the least.

"He's asked me to marry him, you know," she said as she pried open the tin of tea. "Officially, I mean."

"Oh, Renee, that's wonderful!" Kate stood and went over to give her a hug.

Renee tilted her beautifully coifed head toward Kate and lifted an intricately penciled brow her direction. "I'm not so sure it is."

"I thought you were looking forward to hearing him pop the question."

"Don't get me wrong. I love him, I honestly do, and I believe with all my heart that he loves me, no matter what happened with the sting operation."

She steered Kate back to the table, and they both sat down. "And I would be very good for him, if I do say so myself. Bring him out of his shell, so to speak. Add even more adventure to his life."

Kate hadn't noticed he was in a shell but agreed with the adventure part. Life with Renee would definitely be that.

"And we have so much in common. I am as round the bend as he is about apprehending thugs—you know how helpful I am with mysteries you get tangled up in." She paused. "Sleuthing aside, we both enjoy going to the theater, attending operas, visiting museums, shopping at Harrods . . ."

With the exception of sleuthing and shopping, Kate had never heard Renee mention enjoying any of those activities. Perhaps meeting Collin had brought to the forefront some dormant longings for a different lifestyle.

"In the end," Renee said, "I couldn't bear to leave Copper Mill, and he couldn't bear to leave his life in Oxford."

"I'm sorry," Kate said gently.

Across the kitchen, the teakettle sang out.

"Funny thing is," Renee said softly. "It was Kisses, not Mama, who helped me decide. When all was said and done, Mother said she would live with us in England as long as Collin and I would take her to see the Queen on ceremonial days." She shook her head. "No, it was Little Umpkins who helped me decide."

As if on cue, the Chihuahua raced around the corner, feet scrambling to gain traction on the slick floor. When he reached Renee, she scooped him up and held him close. "He can't seem to get over growling at Collin. And we couldn't have that, could we?" She kissed him on the nose.

Tears filled her eyes. "I never thought love would come to me after . . . ," she sniffled, reaching into her pocket for a lace-edged hankie, "after all my sorrow and loss so many years ago. I almost said yes to Collin, thinking it might erase the sad memories. But I know that's the wrong reason to get married." She took a deep breath.

"Have you told Collin?"

"He'll be terribly hurt, possibly to the point of never getting over it," she said, then added dramatically, "of never getting over *moi*."

Renee finished preparing their tea, and then with great fanfare, she set the teacups and saucers on the table. She sat down across from Kate, and Kisses jumped into Renee's lap, circled a few times, then settled down.

Kate blinked at the little dog. If she hadn't known better, she would have sworn Kisses was smiling as he cocked his head in her direction. She half expected him to wink.

Chapter Thirty-One

Thursday morning, Paul brought in the *Chronicle* and tossed it on the kitchen table as Kate poured their coffee. They sat down across from each other to enjoy reading the latest breaking news in Copper Mill.

"I think today's the last of Livvy's columns in the Tuscany series," Paul said, picking up another section.

"That's funny. She hasn't said anything about it." Kate chuckled. "I can only imagine what she's featured this time—probably the apprehension of international thieves at Faith Briar would be my guess."

"*Mm-hmm,*" Paul said, then took a sip of coffee.

Kate opened the paper to Livvy's article. As her eyes scanned down the page, Kate was pleased to see that Livvy had included an extensive account of the dangerous and dramatic conclusion to the capture of the thieves.

"This is so sweet," she told Paul as she pointed to the bottom of the page. "At the end of the article, she says that it's especially wonderful to announce that others from

Copper Mill are about to depart for Tuscany." She looked up, took a sip of coffee, and furrowed her brow. "I wonder who they could be."

"*Hmm* . . . ," Paul said from behind his section of the newspaper.

"She says again there's no more glorious or romantic place to enjoy a second honeymoon, and that all her love and prayers go with this special couple."

"She must know them well to write so warmly about them," Paul said.

"I wonder if she'll actually announce who it is."

Paul put down his paper. "Is there more?"

> It is a joy to announce that the Reverend Paul and Mrs. Kate Hanlon will be enjoying a second honeymoon while on a ten-day tour of Italy that will include Rome, Florence, and Assisi, plus several romantic days "under the Tuscan sun," tucked away in one of the most picturesque B and Bs imaginable.

Kate's eyes filled, and for a moment, she couldn't speak. "Paul . . . ," she finally managed, "I thought . . . How? . . . When did you?"

He laughed and reached for Kate's hands to draw her to her feet. Then he gathered her into his arms and held her close. "I'll explain how I pulled it off later—the mysterious trips to the travel agency in Pine Ridge, getting all our travel documents in order, transferring funds, letting Livvy and the kids in on it . . ."

He pulled back to look into Kate's eyes. "You know, it wasn't easy to keep a secret from a wife whose sleuthing skills are unequaled in these parts."

Kate grinned.

"I promise to fill you in on every detail. But for now, Mrs. Hanlon, let me just say how much I love you and how much I wanted to share this trip with you . . . alone."

"But—" Kate began.

Paul raised his index finger to her lips and whispered, "Trust me."

About the Author

DIANE NOBLE is the award-winning author of *The Butterfly Farm* and nearly two dozen other published works—mysteries, romantic suspense, historical fiction and nonfiction books for women, including three devotionals and an empty nest survival guide. Diane is a three-time recipient of the Silver Angel Award for Media Excellence and a double finalist for Romance Writers of America's prestigious RITA award for Best Inspirational Fiction. Diane makes her home in Southern California with husband Tom and their two cats. You can stop by Diane's Web site at www.dianenoble.com to catch up on the latest about her books, favorite recipes, crochet patterns and much more.

A Note from the Editors

THIS ORIGINAL BOOK was created by the Books and Inspirational Media Division of Guideposts, the world's leading inspirational publisher. Founded in 1945 by Dr. Norman Vincent Peale and Ruth Stafford Peale, Guideposts helps people from all walks of life achieve their maximum personal and spiritual potential. Guideposts is committed to communicating positive, faith-filled principles for people everywhere to use in successful daily living.

Our publications include award-winning magazines such as *Guideposts* and *Angels on Earth*, best-selling books, and outreach services that demonstrate what can happen when faith and positive thinking are applied in day-to-day life.

For more information, visit us at www.guideposts.com, call (800) 431-2344 or write Guideposts, PO Box 5815, Harlan, Iowa 51593.